Writer, Writer

A Novel

By

Milam McGraw Propst

Writer, Writer

© 2013 Milam McGraw Propst

1st Edition

Cover Design: Summer Paul

Layout: Brian C. Aubitz

ISBN 978-0-9844611-2-7

To find additional works from the author please visit her website at:

MilamMcGrawPropst.com

FUZIONPRINT
www.fuzionprint.com
612-781-2815

To Terry,

I know you're proud
of your talented Summer!
Best wishes,
Milan

Happy
Father's Day 2013

♡ Jo

"Writer, Writer" is dedicated to our grandsons,
Loftin Alan Propst and Emmett James Propst.
These charming little men make our lives so rich,
such fun, and most meaningful.

Writer, Writer

by

Milam McGraw Propst

"Life is a tragedy when seen in close-up, but a comedy in long-shot."

Charlie Chaplin, actor, director, composer (1889-1977)

My signature rock hard biscuits were baking in the oven when sparks popped out from under the skillet. A flicker. A flame. Suddenly, my chicken, swimming in hot grease, took aim at me!

I grabbed a dishcloth and fought back.

Round one went to the chicken as the cloth caught fire.

"Help! Help!!"

No one heard my desperate cries. I attempted to douse the blaze with a large pitcher of sweet tea. As with an offering to ancient gods, mine only fueled the thirsty inferno.

"Heeeeelp, somebody, please!"

"Smother a kitchen fire with," our professor told us. Had she said flour? Or baking powder? Baking soda? Salt? Wishing I'd paid more attention in class, I hurled it all at the flaming bird.

Writer, Writer

Miracle of miracles, it worked. I'd saved the Home Management House from certain destruction. The chicken's charred body parts were afloat in tea. Thickened grease in a paste of white covered the stove, the counter tops, cabinets, and a large section of the surrounding floor.

For my class report, I wrote a colorful description of the catastrophe and landed an "A." Apparently, the instructor needed a good laugh.

I was also taking "Introduction to Journalism" to spend time with my charming boyfriend, now husband, Jamey. Toward the end of the semester, we were assigned a speech, so I spoke about my fire. As is my style, I enhanced the devastation a tiny bit. To be honest, I exaggerated quite a lot.

Charles Scarritt, our professor, seemed amused and invited me to talk to him after class. "I'll be blunt, Miss McGraw. You're wasting your time in home economics. Sign up for Journalism 101. I teach it."

"Thank you, Mr. Scarritt, but I can't."

He pulled his glasses down to the end of his nose and glared at me over the rims. "Why not?"

"I'm terrified of typewriters."

"What?"

"I know it sounds ridiculous, Mr. Scarritt, but I hate machines. I inherited the phobia from my mother."

"Don't you worry, little lady. I understand. You can bring a tablet to class."

I couldn't believe the professor's sympathetic concession. A tablet? Piece of cake!

On the first day of the next semester, I all but skipped to Woods Hall. I walked up the rickety steps of the historic pre-Civil War building, turned the corner, and spotted the thoughtful man at his desk.

"I'm here, Mr. Scarritt. Milam McGraw."

"Yes, Miss McGraw. Welcome."

Every desk had a typewriter. There was no room for my tablet.

Mr. Scarritt, again pulling his glasses down his nose, looked me in the eye, and said, "Gotcha."

I'd jumped from the frying pan into the fire, one which has flickered and blazed for fifty years.

Writer, Writer

Hector House

A fitting habitat for a future writer is living in a haunted house, one painted in dread and peopled with monsters. My surroundings also offered me a glimmer of hope, a whisper of love, and, twice a week, Creola Moon, our maid who told stories.

My first clear memories began when I was approximately three-years-old. Momma, Daddy, my grandmother, and I lived on Hector Avenue in Metarie, a suburb of New Orleans. My mother was an alcoholic-in-training. Her drinking was perfected as I aged from birth to six-years-old.

I'd dubbed my grandmother "B," because Momma called her "Butch." I never asked why, but it does seem peculiar for a daughter to call the woman who gave her life by such an unendearing name. It's too late now, but I wish I knew the reason. It might make a good story.

Our dreary, musty bungalow was built from cold yellow stone. It had a screened front porch. A squeaky, squawking ceiling fan in the center hung low threatening any tall person who ventured inside.

"Enter at your own risk," I imagined the fan to say as its blades whipped around in menacing circles. Ceiling fans will always disturb me. They tend to circulate disquieting memories.

Writer, Writer

Our living quarters were on the second story above a dank, dark basement. The living and dining rooms stretched across the front. Momma's kitchen was located behind the dining room with my parent's bedroom behind the living room. My grandmother's room and mine were across from one another in the back. We all shared one bath with a floor made from black and white hexagon-shaped tiles with cracks which made me think of spider webs.

An evil ghost monster lived in the coal bin just below where I slept. My baby bed had a gate which, until I turned three, was closed over me at bedtime and locked. I trusted it to keep me safe from whatever lived in the basement. I can close my eyes and recall, oddly but fondly, the secure feeling of that wooden roof over my bed. I still see its shiny brass latch which served as my guardian.

Later on in life, as I was becoming a writer, our house became a perfect metaphor for the terror and confusion surrounding me.

Creola Moon was the first person to acknowledge my fears. She was a saving grace for me. B, my heart and my protector by night, worked downtown all day. Daddy traveled throughout the South for weeks at a time. Momma, in the infancy of her alcoholism, preferred drinking to mothering me. I thank the Good Lord I had B every night and Creola on Tuesdays and Thursdays. With them, my loneliness melted away as did the terror.

White-haired Creola was kind and fat and smiled like Louis Armstrong, all teeth and jubilation. She was gifted with a vivid imagination, which she eagerly shared with me. I became a sponge soaking up every word she uttered. I've told stories throughout my life, because I learned at the knee of Creola Moon.

"Mary Milam," she moaned, "He's a comin' up from dat coal bin. He gonna eat us alive."

"Creola!" I snuggled between her fat bosoms. "Hold me!"

Creola backed off as much as I'd allow. She took a deep, heavy breath.

"Listen, you hear somethin'?"

"No, surely not, Creola?" I stammered. "Yes, I do!"

She tapped her foot in rhythm on the hardwood floor. "Dat ghost walkin' be gettin' closer, baby girl."

"Oh, Creola!"

"Best not tell you no mo. I don't want my baby be scared."

"Keep on telling. Please!"

"Get youself ready 'cause he's comin' closer, and closer, and closer, *stomp*, *stomp*, and closer, *stomp*."

I wanted to squeeze myself deep inside the benevolent black lady. I yearned to be safe within her.

"Closer and closer, *stomp, stomp*."

Writer, Writer

I could scarcely let out a breath. I swelled up from trying.

Creola grabbed me.

"Gotcha!"

We both screamed and laughed until we hurt. I laughed out of hysteria, and she laughed because of me. To us, there was no question about the existence of the coal bin ghost monster. It was especially evident after the ghoul pushed my grandmother down the basement steps.

It happened on a Saturday afternoon. A rare event, Momma, Daddy, and I went to Lake Pontchartrain for a picnic. B decided to stay behind saying she was exhausted from her job at the law firm.

"I wish I could go with you," B explained, "but I must rest up for work next week."

I begged and begged, but she would not give in. I realize as I've aged, the glare from the lake would have aggravated her old tired eyes. Upon returning home, we found my grandmother in the kitchen. She was holding an ice pack on her forehead. Her right arm lay swelling and lifeless on a soft pillow atop the table.

"B!" I shrieked.

"I'm perfectly fine, little darling. I don't want you to worry."

Our kitchen table was a cursed piece of furniture.

A few weeks prior to B's fall, my mother had cut her hand on the broken glass of a mayonnaise jar. Her blood mingled with the mayo and splattered on the table's shiny white surface. Even though the table top had been wiped clean, I still saw Momma's bright red blood rippling through the creamy yellow mayonnaise.

I, too, had a turn on the table.

I was playing hide and seek with my neighborhood chums, Francie and Jeannie. It was near dinner time, and their mothers would soon be calling them home.

"One last game," I begged.

"Okay, it's my turn to be it," said Francie. "Ten, nine, eight, seven, six." Rushing to find a place to hide, I scooted under the living room sofa. Poised perfectly was a rusty nail laying in wait to puncture my leg.

"The monster stabbed me!"

Momma came running and called the doctor. He arrived in minutes.

"My poor baby," she swooned. "Your pretty little leg is ruined."

They put me on that kitchen table where Momma held me tenderly but tightly. In and out went the doctor's needle like those on B's sewing machine, only much slower. How I wished I'd been a doll's dress instead of a little girl, so his clumsy stitches wouldn't have hurt so bad.

Writer, Writer

Momma went to bed early taking along a glass jingling with ice. B let me sleep with her in her big bed. It was such a treat, I almost forgot about the rusty nail, the pain, and the fact my pretty leg was forever ruined. I do have a scar on my left thigh, but only a small one. My mother taught me well the valuable skill of exaggeration.

After those two gruesome events, I dreaded sitting at that table. I would push food around my plate only pretending to eat.

On the afternoon of my grandmother's accident, the table became a scary stage where I watched her suffer. B didn't let on, but I knew she was being brave for my sake. The swollen knot on her forehead made her look like she was wearing a frightful Mardi Gras mask.

Momma stayed with me while Daddy took my grandmother to the hospital. She was wonderful the whole evening. We read stories and snuggled in my parent's bed. I felt guilty enjoying Momma while B might have needed me.

As it turned out, her arm was badly broken, and she had to miss work for more than two weeks. On a positive note, I was allowed to stay home from Mrs. Bleuler's Kindergarten to take care of her. It made me feel better about not going to the hospital.

"I can't be Butch's nurse," said Momma.

My mother didn't approve of anyone being sick.

"Some people enjoy poor health," she explained. "I don't, Mary Milam. I don't want you to either."

Momma was wrong about one thing. I did enjoy someone's poor health; I enjoyed B's. While Momma listened to her soap operas and drank toddies, B and I both enjoyed her poor health. I relished our time together. We played with my dolls, read, and drew pictures. Naturally, I did anything which required an un-casted right arm.

"We're making the best of a bad situation, little darling," she'd say.

B and I did a lot of looking on the brighter sides of things. Like my father, my grandmother chose to be positive, another good trait for a writer to acquire. It helps when dealing with rejection slips.

My grandmother insisted she'd slipped on the hall rug causing her to fall down the steps. Creola maintained her accident was the direct result of B's disbelief in the coal bin ghost monster.

I listened from the hallway as Creola tried to convince her.

"I jus' know it be true. Dat ghost be out to show his power usin' his meanness to you!"

"That's rubbish, Creola!"

I peeked though the keyhole and saw Creola shaking her head.

Writer, Writer

"You best be careful, ma'am. Watch yo' words. He be listenin' right dis minute!"

I could tell B and Creola were getting into an argument. I heard Momma's program playing on the living room radio and ran to get her. To me, grownups' fighting was far worse than any monster.

Poor Momma, she must have been real tired, because she was sound asleep on our sofa, the same sofa which took the plug out of my leg. Disappointed, I walked tentatively back down the hall and put my ear to the kitchen door.

"Once and for all, Creola, I simply made a misstep. I forbid you to scare my little granddaughter with your foolish suspicions. Coal bin monster, indeed! The child will be terrified."

I burst into the kitchen.

"I am not scared, B. He did push you down the steps. I may have to fight that mean ole monster myself!"

"Lord, have mercy," said Creola. Not knowing where else to put her arms, she threw them up toward Heaven. What I really needed was my dear Creola's arms around me.

As calm as the tranquil pond in our nearby park, my grandmother smiled assuringly at me. She brushed my brown hair back from my eyes and snapped my barrette into place.

"Sweet child, there are no such things as monsters and ghosts, or anything of the kind."

B's wrinkles sank in deep around her eyes. She glared at Creola, flashing the angriest look I'd ever seen on her face.

Then she smiled sweetly at me. Her wrinkles softened.

"You are safe, Milam."

"I am safe."

"Creola Moon is safe. Isn't that right, Creola?"

"Of course, my baby's be safe. Little Milam know it, too. She ain't scared. She knows she's protected 'cause I sees to it!"

Relieved, I let out a breath.

Momma stumbled into the kitchen. "What's this damn commotion?"

"Nothing, Momma."

"Not a thing, Mary Catherine."

"We's all fine, Mrs. McGraw."

Momma went to her room and slammed the door.

Thinking back on their relationship, Creola never could understand B, anymore than my grandmother could understand her. Our maid knew what an intelligent woman my grandmother was so B's failure to comprehend what, to Creola, was God's own truth, must have been inconceivable. I believe Creola regarded B with compassion, and, perhaps, even with pity.

What I do know for certain is they both had my best interests at heart.

I studied the people who loved me. I wondered how they could be so different inside and out. Without intending to do so, they were teaching me indispensable lessons in character study.

My grandmother's arm remained in a cast up over her elbow. The knot on her forehead, though shrinking, stayed black and blue with yellowing edges for days. I needed to do something to help. Mustering my courage, I stood at the top of the basement steps and pushed the door slightly ajar.

Squeeeeeek.

Panic gripped me. Would Creola's protection be effective even when she wasn't beside me?

Swallowing hard I whispered, "Mr. Ghost Monster, are you down there? If you are, please listen. Creola and I believe in you. We beg you to leave my grandmother alone. B can't help how she is; she's too old to learn new things."

I tossed a piece of B's butterscotch down the stairs. I hoped whatever lived in the coal bin had a sweet tooth.

Yahootie Men

From time to time, strange people walked in through our front door. One was a man named Peggy, a perfume shop owner from the French Quarter. He was the first person I'd met, other than Santa Claus, who had a beard. Because it was late summer, I knew Santa was far away making toys at the North Pole. I crawled up in Daddy's lap and whispered a question in his ear.

"Peggy's beard is called a goatee," explained Daddy.

"Goat tea?" I queried.

Peggy chuckled. "Oui, oui, little one, goat tea! But make mine a bourbon, will you, Bill?"

I hoped my daddy wouldn't grow hair on his face. I didn't want him to tickle me with his good night kisses.

Another friend of our family was the tallest man I ever saw up close. Bruce was one person who had to duck, so he'd not be chopped in two by our porch fan. He was super skinny, which made him appear even taller. Bruce was a walking, talking version of Daddy's Yahootie men.

"Please, Daddy, draw me a Yahootie."

"Anything you say, Milam. But first, get me the tools."

I was prepared. I reached behind the sofa and handed him a pencil and tablet.

Writer, Writer

As I watched, Daddy sketched out a stick figure with long
fingers and toes. He added a bowtie and topped his drawing
with a stovepipe hat like Abraham Lincoln's.

"More, more," I applauded.

"Okay, let's see how many I can draw before
dinner."

A dozen men later, Momma called to me from the
kitchen. I hurried to show her Daddy's drawings.

"My goodness, Milam, the Yahooties remind me of
Bruce."

"Momma, they do! But without his disguise."

"Disguise?"

"His white mask."

"That's a medical mask to keep us safe from his
bug."

"Bug?"

"You remember, Milam, our friend has that awful
cough."

I filled the grownups' glasses with ice. After I
carried my milk to the dining room, I went back to
Momma.

"Is Bruce's wife a fortune teller?"

"No, of course not! Why would you think such a
thing about Janeece?"

"Because her hair is blacker than my chalkboard, and she wears a hundred gold bracelets up and down both her arms."

Momma laughed, "Mary Milam McGraw, you can come up with the most outrageous notions."

B was standing at the sink rinsing off lettuce, listening. The next time Bruce and Janeece came over; she took me to the park. My grandmother wasn't afraid of much, but she hated bugs.

I liked our eccentric visitors with the exception Daddy's co-worker from the Linde Company.

"I want you to call me Uncle Bob."

Sometimes I would, but I didn't want to. He was not my uncle.

When he came to see us, Bob would perform magic tricks. One time, he took a drag from a long black cigarette holder and quickly dipped his holder into a bowl of sudsy water. To my delight, Bob blew zillions of soap-filled bubbles. I danced around popping the bubbles while he roared with laughter.

Bob also drew pictures but not of Yahooties like my daddy's. His drawings were far more intricate. He once mailed me a letter in an envelope crafted to look exactly like a streetcar. Eight stamps across the front became passengers.

Writer, Writer

Bob liked streetcars so much he purchased a used one from the city of New Orleans. Converting it into a house for himself, he parked his trolley-home on the banks of Lake Pontchartrain.

Bob took many, many photographs of me, mostly out in our backyard near the banana trees. One afternoon when he was taking my picture, Momma got really mad at him about something I didn't quite understand. She never let him visit us again. Not too long afterwards, Bob died in his streetcar.

I liked the Yahootie men, Peggy and Bruce, but not Bob.

I loved Daddy, who created Yahooties for me.

I loved Momma for making Bob go away.

More Strange Happenings

We had two exceptionally bizarre weather related calamities at our house. First, the water in our toilet froze.

"Damndest thing I ever saw," shouted my father early on Saturday morning. "How could the water in a toilet bowl freeze like that?"

"Daddy, it was the coal bin ghost monster."

"Milam, what an imagination you have! I think our problem has more to do with Mother Nature."

I prayed Mother Nature hadn't moved into our basement.

While my father contacted the plumber, I pitched candy down the steps.

The spring I turned five, we had a terrible storm. It thundered as if the angry sky was knocking to come inside. Lightening boomed and lit my room brighter than day. I grabbed my teddy bear, ran, and jumped into B's bed. The whole house was jiggling like Momma's raspberry Jell-O, but this was the opposite of our favorite dessert. The earsplitting noise and shaking continued as B and I clung onto one another.

KKKAAABAM! The top of our giant oak tree broke off and crashed through the roof into the front of our house. Massive branches stretched their long limbs down the hall only feet from where B and I were huddled. Rain and hail pounded all the harder. B and I screamed at the top of our lungs, but I couldn't hear my grandmother's voice or even my own, because the storm shouted all the louder with its deafening thunder and rapid fire cracks of lightening. I clung tighter to B wishing she weren't so skinny. I yearned for Creola's body to shield me.

Thank goodness my father wasn't out of town on business. He called to us, "I'll be right there. I'm phoning for help."

"Hurry, Daddy, we're real scared!"

"Be brave, Milam," said B, hugging me tighter. "I've got you."

"Stay put, you two," said my daddy.

From my grandmother's bed, I could see Momma shuddering as she wrapped her blue silk robe around herself. She hung onto Daddy while he dialed the telephone. His voice was quaking.

"Hello, fire department?"

Daddy came in and scooped me up in his strong arms. "You're safe."

I wanted to believe him, but I couldn't. Just then, the brutal storm bellowed yet another loud threat; and I squeezed his neck.

In the distance, we heard sirens. The fire trucks were on their way!

B put her robe around me and grabbed an umbrella. Daddy carried me, and we made our way out through the kitchen and down the back steps.

Flashing red lights radiated Hector Avenue. I screamed, "Yippeeee!"

My father rushed to greet the firemen, while Momma, B, and I stood under her umbrella. It felt like the movies when the U.S. Calvary arrived. Except, these men had no horses, only red trucks. In the excitement, I rallied, and all five-years-old of me embraced the chaos. I never dreamed there could be so many people coming to see about my family.

As soon as the worst of the hard rain let up, neighbors arrived with more umbrellas, hot coffee, and blankets. The Fishers took us next door to their home, but none of us got back to sleep. The next morning, as soon as the sun came up, we walked back across the driveway to check out the damage. What we saw stunned even the grownups. Only a few recognizable pieces of furniture stuck out from an enormous tangle of limbs and leaves, soggy wet rubble, roofing shingles, boards, broken concrete, and all manner of nasty muck.

"Can you fix this, Daddy?"

"I don't know, Honey. I hope so."

Writer, Writer

Daddy was always an optimist. If I had a dime for every time he said, "Darkest before the dawn," I'd be a wealthy woman today. Trying to comfort me, my father gathered himself.

"Don't worry, Milam. Everything will turn out fine. I promise."

"Pinky promise?"

Daddy wrapped his big finger around mine and said, "Pinky promise, Honey."

I latched onto his finger.

"There's one thing for sure," he added, "I won't have as many leaves to rake next fall."

As our neighbors and other friends came over, I watched with Francie and Jeannie from a safe distance. B insisted.

"Were you scared?" asked Francie.

"Nope."

"You're really brave."

"The best part was when the fire trucks came," I bragged, basking in their rapt attention. "Must have been twenty trucks and a hundred firemen."

"Wow."

"Milam, you're so lucky!"

The grownups combed though broken furniture, pictures, Momma's radio, and rain soaked rugs and pillows.

A mountain of trash filled our yard. A bunch of junk had
fallen in from the attic. I rescued my stuffed Santa Claus.

"B, look what's happened to Santa."

"Give him to me, little darling. I'll clean him for
you."

Momma cried as she picked up shattered pieces of
her china. I ran over to where she was sitting Indian style
with broken bits of porcelain in her lap.

"I'm sorry, Momma."

"It's okay, sweetie. I'm relieved none of us were
hurt. Especially you."

I started to cry. Momma cared more about us than
she did her dishes. Of course, I knew I was important to
her. Sometimes, it was just nice to hear her say so. Momma
tossed aside the broken china and pulled me into her lap.
She was holding on to me tighter than when the doctor
stitched my leg.

B went back to work the very next day. She never
let anything get in the way of her responsibilities. A benefit
of the fallen tree was my parents were so busy getting
things cleaned and repaired Momma didn't drink toddies,
and Daddy didn't leave town for three entire weeks.

My father was right, good things do come from bad.
I was becoming an optimist, too. Why not, after all, wasn't
I my daddy's little girl? I wanted to be exactly like Bill
McGraw. I was my happiest when he was at home.

Writer, Writer

Daddy's little girl always slept better when he was there for a good night kiss.

Two days later, I found Santa on my bed. He was as fresh and clean as the Christmas morning he appeared under our tree. I was B's little girl, too.

B's Wardrobe

The last creepy and most terrifying Hector happening took place in my grandmother's bedroom. B had an enormous piece of furniture, one which she treasured and referred to as her "wardrobe." Its three-way folding mirror was anchored on a mahogany base. The twelve-foot-tall piece ran the length of her room and held five drawers where she kept her nighties and unmentionables.

I was alone in her room coloring at the foot of her bed when I felt a cold chill. I sensed someone watching me. Slowly, I looked up.

"Momma?"

It wasn't my mother. I could hear her in the kitchen. I shuddered. A second chill ran down my back. I turned toward my grandmother's wardrobe. Out of the corner of my eye, as sure as I could be, I caught a glimpse of an animal. It was looking at me from inside the center panel. In my vivid writer's memory, it was something black with vicious teeth, yellow eyes, and a bright red tongue. It looked like a wolf!

I threw down my crayon and bolted from B's room. My feet hardly touched the floor.

"Momma!"

"A scary wolf with sharp teeth!" I shrieked as I tried to describe the horrifying beast.

Writer, Writer

"Don't be silly, Milam McGraw, there's nothing there," said Momma. She took a puff of her cigarette and continued to stir a pot of tomato soup.

"Was, too!"

"Milam, for Pete's sakes," she laughed. "You're letting your imagination get the best of you."

I turned and muttered under my breath. I stormed outside and waited on the porch steps for the city bus to bring B home. An hour later, I spotted her coming from eight houses down the street. I ran to meet her.

"B, there's the awfulest wolf living in your mirror! I saw him, sure as can be, but Momma doesn't believe me."

My grandmother, calm and steady as always, asked if I might have had another bad dream.

B and I knew all about nightmares, because we had more than our share. My worst one occurred around Thanksgiving. I dreamed I was hiding in a fort when a dinosaur came inside and ate me. The funny thing was I was made out of turkey stuffing!

My grandmother's weren't silly. So dreadful were hers, B's screaming would wake up everyone in our house. Momma or Daddy had to go shake her awake, because she screamed so loud. B's nightmares used to scare me, but I eventually got accustomed to them. I'd roll over and put the pillow over my ears until she quit hollering.

As an adult, when I learned about my grandfather's death, it became evident B's screaming had nothing to do with dinosaurs. The grieving woman's nightmares came from reliving the horrendous afternoon her husband committed suicide. She and my mother found him near the wardrobe.

B and I walked hand in hand down Hector. "Tell me again, exactly what did you see?"

I repeated my story about the wolf in the mirror. She didn't act surprised; B trusted every word I said. She always insisted my imagination was a gift.

"Little darling," she advised, "Put the wolf out of your mind. If you don't think about him, he will disappear. Do you understand?"

"Yes, I think so. I'll try."

We walked under the ceiling fan. My grandmother put down her purse and placed her hands on my shoulders.

"Promise you won't look in that mirror again. Your resolve will scare him away. Promise?"

"I promise."

"Now, off with you. Let me go see about your mother."

I went to the backyard and stretched myself out on Daddy's gravel pile. I'd carved a deep chasm which cradled my whole body. Nearly every afternoon, I would lie there and sing as I watched the sun go down.

I almost broke my promise once. I tiptoed into B's room and tried to force myself to look in the mirror. I edged slowly around the door frame and tilted my head toward her wardrobe, but I stopped in my tracks.

Was it my promise to my grandmother or was fear holding me back? For whatever reason, I never risked even a quick peek. I didn't want my imagination to kick in, if what I saw was my budding creativity at work.

A few months later Daddy got transferred to Memphis, and my parents put our house on the market. As part of the sale, my grandmother included her prized wardrobe. She did not mention the wolf. I was worried about the new family, so I pitched one last piece of candy down the stairs.

"Whoever you are, please don't frighten the children."

I was more than happy to leave the house on Hector Avenue. At the same time, I was heartbroken about saying good bye to people I loved.

I fell to pieces on Creola's last day.

"What will I do without you!" I wailed.

"Be strong is what you do, Mary Milam. See these eyes of mine? I still be watchin' over you when you be's in

Memphis. You shut tight your own eyes and knows ole' Creola is a lovin' you. And, Chil, don't you be forgettin' our stories."

She turned and started down our back steps, righted her hat, and walked away.

I ran after Creola, but she waved me off. "Chil, I say be strong!"

I took myself to Daddy's rock pile and burrowed in as deep as I could.

To make things more painful, my grandmother stayed behind in New Orleans.

"Don't you worry, little darling, I'll move to Memphis before you can turn around."

"Promise?"

"I promise."

I turned around and around and around again.

With Daddy already gone, Momma and I locked up the house and took a taxi to the railroad station. We were supposed to have a good time on our train ride to Memphis, but I ruined everything. I cried off and on throughout the entire trip. My mother was clearly disappointed.

"For Pete's sakes, Milam, where's your spirit of adventure?"

"I'm having a wonderful time, Momma." I blew my nose.

Writer, Writer

Momma ordered drinks, a Coke for me and for herself, a toddy.

It took five long months before B finally arrived in Memphis. During that time, we added on extra space for her. Upon seeing her new apartment, she said, "It is lovely, Mary Catherine, Bill. I couldn't be happier."

I couldn't have been happier either. It was bad enough doing without Creola, but I could not have survived losing my grandmother forever.

Were I writing a happy ending to our family's story, it would have gone something like this: Momma, Daddy, and I moved into our nice new home in Tennessee. B came to Memphis on the very next train and brought Creola with her, and my mother stopped drinking forever.

My mother did not stop drinking, and I never saw Creola Moon again.

Memphis

We settled into our place on Montclair Drive. Sadly for us and for herself, Momma got worse. Her drinking altered the way she treated us, especially how she treated my father. I would start feeling anxious as the change slowly crept over her. Alcohol turned my mother into a cursing beast.

"Don't be afraid, Honey," said Daddy. "Your mother is talking in a foreign language. It's French."

I let on like I believed him. I wanted to believe every word my father said, but Momma's spiteful words were definitely not French.

I could tell my mother was getting drunk because her face turned red. Her eyes would squint to almost shut, and her jaw started to twist. I came up with a plan. If I couldn't hear or see my mother's rage, maybe like the wolf in B's wardrobe, it didn't exist. I would quickly retreat to my room and play with my Roy Rogers ranch set, scribble stories on a tablet, or run outside to my swings and pump until my toes touched the clouds. Denial at the tender age of six turned into food for my expanding imagination and my appetite for writing. I also started to look for the brighter side in bad situations. One evening as I pumped high on my swing, two things dawned on me. With B's help, I made a list.

#1 The wolf is gone.

Writer, Writer

#2 No houses on Montclair Drive have basements. No coal bins. No monsters.

Santa brought me a shiny blue bike for Christmas. Two weeks later Daddy removed the training wheels.

"Are you sure you're ready for this?"

"Yes, Daddy."

He and I took "Spitfire" to the highest end of our back yard. My father steadied me. I gripped the handle bars as he gave me a gentle shove. Wobbly at first, I took off and sailed the whole length of our big yard. I felt the wind in my hair and never again required his help or the support of those extra wheels.

Daddy hollered, "That's my girl, you did it!"

"Yes, I did!"

Freedom! For the next eight years, I would ride my bike in ever enlarging circles farther and farther away from our house.

An advantage of being raised by an alcoholic, a traveling business man, and a working grandmother, I was free to explore anywhere I chose. I rode to the homes of friends, to the drugstore on Highpoint Terrace, to Daddy's golf course at Colonial Country Club, and to neighborhoods miles away from Montclair Drive.

Another advantage was I got to experience great adventures. Some of the excitement was due to Momma's drinking companion. Her name was Gin. A glamorous woman, Gin was tall, with a shock of prematurely white hair, and a contagious laugh. Her appearance was in stark contrast to Momma's. The two women were equally beautiful, but my mother was petite with soft blond hair and blue eyes.

Gin and Momma repeatedly took Gin's daughter Jo and me out with them. We'd go to Overton Park for a picnic and stay for hours on end. When Momma and Gin bought their beer or other drinks of their choice, Jo and I were treated to multiple scoops of ice cream. I am not being a "damn Pollyanna" as my mother used to say. It's the simple truth. Jo and I, along with Momma and Gin, had many an exciting time together.

One of our best experiences was the Halloween when Jo and I were ten. Ours was the prime age for Trick or Treat. Momma and Gin were focused on their party which would last most of the night. The result was we girls, dressed as gypsies, trick or treated in their neighborhood until well after 10 p.m. My own enormous bag of candy lasted for three months.

I shared my Hershey bars with Momma. She always loved chocolate.

Writer, Writer

My mother occasionally filled in as my accomplice in mischief. After a few sips of vodka, she became uninhibited. Bored one afternoon, the two of us decided to make a heist. We sneaked over to our snooty neighbor's back porch. At Momma's urging, I grabbed the woman's bejeweled gold bedroom slippers, ran, and hurled the shoes into our bamboo grove.

"Mrs. Pruneface will never know it was us," she laughed as we spied on the woman's house.

"Are you sure?" I fretted.

"Who cares anyway?" replied my mother with heightened glee.

"Mrs. Pruneface is nothing but an old prude." My mother's voice got louder as she stuck her thumbs in her ears, wiggled her fingers, and yelled, "You prune-faced frump!"

"What's a frump, Momma? A prude? I don't know those words. Are they French?"

"Frumps and prudes are people who never have fun," she explained. "Milam, don't you dare turn into a frump or a prude. Do you hear me? I don't want you to be boring."

"I promise, Momma. I'll never, ever, ever act like a frump or a prude."

"That's my girl."

I became my mother's daughter.

That evening, B helped me write down the two new words in my pink diary.

Momma bought Mrs. Pruneface brand new gold slippers.

My B

Throughout the next eight years beginning in 1951, my grandmother caught the Highpoint Terrace bus and rode downtown to her job at the Ellis Auditorium. How much time and energy had B poured into me when she had so little left for herself? Dwelling in my own world as an egocentric child, it never occurred to me how exhausted my grandmother must have been after her long days as the executive secretary for Chauncey Barbour. By day, Mr. Barbour's efficient secretary was on duty for him. By night, the same lady summoned every molecule of her strength for me.

Every other Saturday, B went in for a half day's work. Once I turned ten, she let me come downtown to meet her for lunch. Feeling all grown up, I'd catch her bus and ride by myself to the auditorium. My grandmother would be standing out front waving as I stepped off.

"Hey, B!"

"Hello, little darling. Did you have fun on the bus?"

Writer, Writer

"I always do. You're so lucky, B. You get to ride every day."

"Lucky am I, Milam?" she replied. "I am lucky to have you."

My grandmother took me by the hand as we began our traditional walk down Main Street. I delighted in gazing up at the tall buildings. She and I always took a turn through the historic park known as Court Square.

All those years and years ago, a small seed was planted for stories about my grandmother's childhood, a time when she was known not as B, but as Ociee Nash. I wrote about downtown Memphis in the third of the five-book series. In the story, on an Easter Sunday in the early 1900's, her older brother, Fred took an eleven-year-old Ociee and their twelve-year-old brother Ben for a horse and buggy ride. A stop along their way was Court Square.

"May we stop here, B?"

"Of course, here's a nickel for you to throw in the fountain. Don't forget to make a wish."

She and I both understood what mine would be. I pitched the coin and prayed for Momma to be sober when we got home.

Even though B and I discussed trying new restaurants, we usually ended up at Walgreens lunch counter. Once we did dine at Hotel Chisca but regretted doing so. The meal didn't measure up to our high standards. Walgreens offered fizzy fountain drinks with finely crushed ice. I'd get mine with a bright red cherry, the perfect complement for our grilled cheeses on white.

"After we finish, shall we go shopping?"

"Do you really think we could?" I only acted surprised. Buying my souvenir was a significant part of our routine.

"Certainly, I have my eye on another animal for your collection."

"Yippee! Are we going to Woolworth's?"

"Where else?"

Today, should our house catch fire, in my list of items to rescue, are three tiny brown rubber bears, a yellow poodle, a duck, a panda, and a monkey with a derby hat. Each stands just over one inch tall. B helped me select every one of them.

Daddy was gone most week days, and Momma was often asleep on the sofa. It was up to my grandmother and me to prepare our dinners. B was tired from her job but insisted I get started on my homework while she cooked. "Cooked" is a relative term. Our meals were quick and simple. She prepared her famous peanut butter sandwiches with either orange marmalade or strawberry jelly. To introduce variety, she would substitute the jelly with a sliced tomato and mayonnaise, but only if tomatoes were in season. Sometimes B would mix sweet pickle relish with peanut butter and stir in a teaspoon of mayonnaise. It is important to note, mayonnaise was the key ingredient. Not only did it add a tasty zing, but it also kept the peanut butter from sticking to her dentures.

My grandmother loved mayonnaise almost as much as she loved me.

What we ate mattered little to me. What was important was the blessed security I experienced sitting at B's two-person table. Only three rooms and a hall away from the sofa where Momma was passed out, my grandmother's apartment offered an oasis of calm. After dinner, I'd finish my homework while B tended to her mending. Having her close, hearing my spelling words, applauding my paragraphs, or flipping math flash cards made life bearable.

Taste of Success

Neither a talented athlete nor a confident dancer, I zeroed in on writing as soon as I learned how to properly hold a pencil. B was my first and most constant encourager.

"Little darling, read me what you've written."

I could have penned "I picked my nose today," and my grandmother would clap for my creative effort. She'd then hand me a tissue with a word of warning about having better manners.

In second grade at St. Agnes Academy, I'd composed a poem titled "The Christmas Mouse." To my surprise, Sister Agnes Ricarda submitted my work to our school's newspaper "The Aquila."

My poem was chosen! I can still feel the supreme satisfaction of seeing the byline "by Mary Milam McGraw." Good grades, finally making the basketball team, earning a scholarship, having the lead in the eighth grade play, and performing in numerous dance recitals not withstanding, my poem's appearing in "The Aquila" was the highlight of my eight years at St. Agnes.

I still had to deal with my situation at home. One downside of living with my family was growing up with virtually no discipline. Although I thought of my freedom as a positive most of the time, I did feel strangely envious of other children. I yearned for rules. Whenever my friends and I were mischievous, I was simply sent home. When my favorite playmates, Mary Catherine and Margaret or their younger sisters Elizabeth and Virginia Harrison got spankings, they were immediately comforted by their caring mother with significant cuddling.

I missed being cuddled.

Sometimes, I'd even pretend to be punished.

"I got into trouble this weekend," I announced to my classmate, Carol. "Daddy discovered holes in his tool room wall."

"Holes?"

"Yes, Margaret and I were playing *Annie Oakley*. We needed to spy on the bad guys, so I got out his drill and bored peepholes."

"My father would have killed me for getting into his stuff!"

"Daddy wanted to kill me, too. He sent me to my room for hours and hours without dinner."

In truth, my father said nothing. Not wanting to hurt my feelings during our short time together, Daddy repaired the damage with wood putty. Maybe, just maybe, he suggested I leave his tools alone. In some ways, I was spoiled rotten.

One especially artistic adventure involved another classmate, Florence. She and I'd enjoyed a delightful afternoon ravaging her mother's extensive clothes closet. We giggled and paraded about in her parent's lavish master bedroom joyfully modeling Mrs. Robinson's fur coats, jewelry, and Cotton Carnival ballgowns.

Unexpectedly, Florence's mother appeared.

"What in the world are you girls doing?"

Seeing her finery strewn all about, Mrs. Robinson's face turned as red as Momma's. Yelling, she came after Florence. She grabbed a hairbrush from her dressing table and pulled my friend across her lap. It wasn't my friend's hair but her bottom which received Mrs. Robinson's attention.

I raced home on my bike. For once, I wasn't jealous. I was terrified witnessing another mother's rage.

I might have turned into a horrid little girl, but instead I resolved to discipline myself. It was important for me to please others. I especially wanted to please my mother. If I behaved perfectly, perhaps she would, too.

On occasion, she did.

For my tenth birthday Momma took me shopping at Lowenstein's Department Store. A fifteen-minute bike ride from our house, I'd peddled Spitfire past the store's beautiful display windows many a day never dreaming I'd ever be a customer.

Writer, Writer

On that extraordinary afternoon, Momma and I selected twin quilted bedspreads with a pattern of pink roses.

"Momma, these look like the roses in our yard. I'll pretend yours climbed inside through my window."

"Milam, what a sweet idea."

We were having a glorious time. My mother was showing me the matching dust ruffles and café curtains when the saleslady came up.

"Dusty pink," she said.

"Dusty? Don't you have any clean ones? After all, this is my birthday present."

The lady chuckled. "My dear, I'm referring to the color "dusty pink." These items are brand new, and I can assure you they are quite clean."

"Oh."

I spotted an adorable corduroy chair. With the saleslady's permission, I sat down to try it out.

"Momma, this chair fits me. Could we please buy it?"

"Of course, we can. Besides, it matches the dirty pink curtains."

I caught her joke. We giggled, Momma and I. After a second, so did the saleslady.

My redecorated bedroom was one of my best presents ever.

Years later, I lovingly had the chair reupholstered for my mother's retirement apartment. The same small chair now graces the room of our grandson, Emmett.

Palmetto

Daddy took me to Florida every summer. He went for business and to visit his parents, Ethel and Will McGraw. I joyfully went along to spend time with him and with our Florida family. My grandparents lived in Palmetto in a large white house on the shores of the Manatee River. In the winter time, Grandma rented two upstairs apartments to the snowbirds from Canada. She liked earning extra money for herself. During the summer months, the whole house belonged to us.

Sometimes Daddy and I would drive to Sarasota to visit our cousins, the Smiths, who lived at Lido Beach. I looked forward to swimming with their son, Melvin. In my mind, he was the luckiest kid on earth to have the Gulf of Mexico right across the street. We always drove back to Palmetto after our morning swims because Grandma loved to cook for my daddy.

In the evenings, we'd sit on the screened porch and talk. Sometimes I listened, but mostly I asked questions. My grandparents had an old metal glider which squeaked when I pumped back and forth. Grandfather got irritated with the noise, while Grandma giggled and winked at me.

"Grandma, why do you call my daddy "Billy Boy" even though he's a grownup?"

"Because he'll always be my little boy, my Billy Boy."

"Daddy, will I always be your little girl?"

"Of course, you will."

"Children do have a way of growing up," Grandma added with a sigh.

It was difficult for me to think of my father as a child. But I could easily imagine myself grown and surrounded by my own family with a Thanksgiving turkey ready to bless and serve.

We listened as crickets chirped.

Fish jumped in the river, and frogs croaked.

"Daddy, do you think we'll see some boats?"

"I don't know why not. We saw three last night. Remember, you were the first to spot the big barge coming under the bridge."

"I like smaller ones better. I can almost wish myself into a me-sized boat smack dab in the middle of the Manatee!"

Adjusting her binoculars, Grandma looked out across the water.

"What are you looking for, Grandma?"

"For interesting water fowl. It's almost dark now, but we just might see a frisky young seagull hurrying back to his nest."

An artist in her own right, Grandma dearly loved collecting sea shells. She made crafts from shells she picked up on the beach. She and I always set aside special time to make something to take back to Momma.

"Keep watch to your left, Honey," said Daddy. "It's almost time for the train."

My McGraw grandparents were natives of Kentucky. Grandfather was a retired L&N Railroad man, as were his six brothers, all of whom had retired to Palmetto.

"Trains are in our blood, Milam."

"In my blood, Daddy?"

"No doubt about it."

When he became a grandfather himself, my daddy couldn't contain his enthusiasm. He insisted on buying his grandsons, William and Jay, a train set well before either was old enough to appreciate his gesture. Little wonder I would eventually write about trains. After all, they are in my blood.

A favorite part of our trips to Florida were the walks Daddy and I took across the bridge connecting Palmetto with Bradenton. I can still feel the grip of my father's hand when cars zipped by.

"Be careful, Milam. Don't step on that stingray!"

Writer, Writer

It was rare to have my father to myself and with no threat of someone ruining our time together. We could talk about everything on the planet, even about Momma. I could always confide in Daddy. During one such walk, I discussed an insurmountable problem I was facing, my height.

"I'm too tall!" I complained.

"You're perfect."

"No, Daddy, I'm not. Remember, Sister made me be St. Joseph in the Christmas pageant again last year. I wanted to be the Blessed Mother, but only short people like Carol get to play Mary."

"You got it from your Uncle Ed," he explained as if I had some dreadful disease.

"Got it?"

"I meant to say you inherited your nice height from my brother. Milam, I think you are a beautiful girl. You'll see, in a few years, I'll be beating off boys with a baseball bat."

I jumped over a flopping fish.

"You really think so?"

"I know so. When we get home, I'm going to buy a whole box of bats."

"A whole box?"

"Yes, maybe two. Now let's get back to Grandma's. There's watermelon waiting for us."

I cannot hear the word "Palmetto" without missing Daddy, especially our walks across the bridge.

Writer, Writer

I Love Lucy

Another special memory from childhood is about my grandmother B.

In my army of dolls, she provided me with an unlikely favorite. Her name is Lucy. B purchased the handmade doll in New Orleans when I was two or three-years-old. Lucy could well be Creola Moon's child. Caramel in color, she has brownish hair fashioned from yarn. Her mouth is a dot of red felt, and her eyes are dots of brown circled in white. Lucy is tiny. Were she able to stand up straight, she would be ten-inches-tall. However, with her curved legs, she must either crawl or sit cross-legged. Lucy's dress is red with white polka dots. My constant companion for years, I carried her with me every place I went. Many were the times we had to turn our car back around, so I could run back inside to fetch her.

Daddy once had to climb more than twenty feet down into the Grand Canyon to rescue her.

"Daddiieeee!" I shrieked. "Lucy blew away when I was taking her picture! You have to save her!"

My father, who was absolutely terrified of heights, immediately went after the doll. Five minutes later, gripping Lucy under his chin, he pulled himself up over of the stacked-rock ledge.

Handing her to me, he exclaimed, "Here's Lucy!"

"Thank you, Daddy! Roy Rogers himself is not as brave as you."

My father looked back over his shoulder and dropped to his knees. Realizing where he'd been, the traumatized man turned ash white. He shook for the remainder of our vacation.

The years had not been good to Lucy. A result of my constant love and attention, her cloth body was becoming frayed as she lingered at death's door.

One evening, I rushed into my grandmother's apartment frantically searching for my doll. She had gone missing for hours.

"B, have you seen Lucy? I'm scared Momma threw her away!"

"She's here, little darling," said B. "Lucy has been visiting with me."

My grandmother pointed to her sewing machine. There sat Lucy looking clean and fresh and sporting a new hairdo.

I picked up my precious doll and kissed her felt lips. "Lucy, you look so very pretty!"

I held her cloth hands making the little doll clap to show my grandmother how much we both appreciated her makeover.

Writer, Writer

"Do you like her hair?" asked B. "I'm afraid the yarn is a bit red, but I couldn't find a better match."

"B, she's perfect. Thank you!"

I wish I could locate someone to redo my doll. But no one else would have my grandmother's caring touch.

Writer, Writer was conceived in a family of dysfunction.

Writer, Writer was also born from a family of gentle moments.

Writing about pleasant memories has been essential for me. As I pen these stories, my heart softens; and the roots of my soul grow deeper.

Writer, Writer

Atlanta

A full blown miracle took place in 1959. My mother finally got herself sober! Her transformation began after my father was transferred to Atlanta, and I entered St. Pius X Catholic High School.

There was a downside. A big one. When Momma, Daddy, and I moved, my grandmother opted to remain in Memphis. Obviously crushed for myself, I was equally concerned about her. What would my precious B do without me?

"Don't you dare worry, little darling," she insisted. "My midtown apartment is much closer to work and will make things easier for me. If you act gloomy, I'll be mad with you."

My grandmother noted her new address was 2186 Monroe, while ours was 2086 Oakawana Road.

"You see," she said circling the numbers. "2186 and 2086, you and I are practically neighbors."

Now a grandmother myself, I cannot imagine how devastated she must have been when my parents and I drove away leaving her alone in her apartment on Monroe. I weep at the memory.

I also ponder B's daily routine for the next ten years. Until she turned eighty-years-old, my grandmother got up early each morning to ready herself for work. She would lock the door of her apartment and walk down the tree lined block to her bus stop at the intersection of Monroe and Madison. No matter how bad the weather, the dear lady stood waiting stoically for the city bus.

The image is etched so deeply in my mind that I see her to this day. There's a photograph at our local deli in which a little old lady stands in an Italian train station. She's so like B it breaks my heart.

On my way to work one rainy morning in 1989, I was stopped at a red light. Out of the corner of my eye, I noticed a thin, elderly lady standing at a bus stop on Roswell Road. Like my grandmother, she was wearing a beige raincoat, flat shoes, and around her neck was tied a dark paisley scarf. Gray-blond hair framed her furrowed face. I sat through the light as drivers behind me honked angrily. My gaze remained fixed on the lady.

Cars continued to honk as the rain pounded on my windshield. I couldn't take my eyes off the mysterious woman, the very image of Mr. Barbour's dependable secretary. Ramrod straight, she never moved. Finally, the bus stopped. She stepped on board and disappeared.

I mouthed the words, "Thank you, B, thank you for the nights you waited in rain to come home to me. Never once did you complain.

Thank you, B, for sending us off to Atlanta without a word of sympathy for yourself.

Writer, Writer

Thank you, B, for being the most unselfish person I ever knew.

Thank you, B, for being my first fan."

The man behind me again blasted his horn. I waved an apology and turned into the traffic. Never again did I see my grandmother's double. I looked for her for weeks.

Writer, Writer

The New Improved Mary Catherine McGraw

Momma faithfully attended daily Mass at Immaculate Heart of Mary Church and served as president of the Altar Society. She bought two dashhounds, Gus and Tinkerbell, took me to and from school until I got my license, and kept company with our gregarious next door neighbor, Lillian Allen.

Daddy wasn't traveling all the time, so we enjoyed family dinners together. After several months of her sobriety, I no longer worried my mother might embarrass me. I entertained friends from school. My spend-the-night parties were legendary as we high school girls spread out on the living room rug, ate junk food, drank Cokes, giggled, and talked about boys. Of course, thanks to Creola Moon, I'd always entertain everyone with a ghost story.

The next morning while he was passing out Krispy Kreme donuts, Daddy teased, "How you can call this a slumber party is a mystery to me. You girls were up talking the whole damn night!"

My father loved every minute. Like me, he was thrilled with Momma's remarkable turnaround. My mother seemed equally happy and even involved herself with my busy social life. She made friends with my classmate's mothers, Frances Putnam, Betty Ann's mother, and with Josephine Murray, Helen's mother.

In early summer of 1961, B came to Atlanta for a long weekend. She left work and boarded a Greyhound bus. Making frequent stops, the trip took the better part of fourteen hours.

The minute Daddy and I walked into the kitchen with my grandmother, Momma said, "Welcome to Atlanta, Butch, I have a surprise for you. Tomorrow, you, Milam, and I are driving to Asheville to find your house on Charlotte Street!"

B dropped her suitcase. "Mary Catherine, let me catch my breath."

This was not the reaction my mother expected. She'd started planning our adventure the very day B's letter arrived to announce her coming.

"Come on, Butch, we'll have a fine time," urged my mother. "Aren't you curious to see the old place?"

"I suppose so."

My grandmother would not consider disappointing her daughter, a daughter trying her best to remain sober. Long accustomed to walking on egg shells around my mother, none of us would have done anything to upset the apple cart.

At the crack of dawn the next morning, B, amazingly rested, complimented Momma on her scrambled eggs; and we were off to the mountains. The day was warm and pleasant as Momma, well schooled in all things that bloom, excitedly pointed out the magnificent rhododendrons and mountain laurels along the Blue Ridge Parkway.

Trying to sound enthusiastic, I said, "The yellow, red, and purple wildflowers are especially pretty, Momma. But I like your roses and irises more."

In her pursuit to show her mother the old Nash family home, Momma drove faster and faster around mountain curves and corkscrew turns. B and I became deathly carsick, but neither of us would let on.

Mary Catherine Whitman McGraw was in her glory.

Three hours later, we pulled up in front of 66 Charlotte Street. To everyone's delight, especially to Momma's, the stately Victorian home had been turned into a florist shop.

"I found it, Butch!" Triumphantly, Momma leapt from the car.

I opened B's door. Our eyes locked. She whispered, "I'm still feeling queasy, little darling."

"Well, aren't you two coming?"

"Momma, B's stomach is bothering her."

Oddly undaunted, my mother got back in the car.

"Butch, let's get a bite of lunch. Maybe that will help."

"I'm sorry, Mary Catherine."

"At least, we saw the house," said my mother. "It's just as well. The drive took longer than I thought. We need to get back to Atlanta before dark."

Momma found a lovely café.

"I enjoyed seeing the place," said B taking a sip of soup.

"I can remember Aunt Mamie sitting at her sewing machine doing her best to teach me how to fashion a blouse. What an unsophisticated little farm girl I must have seemed to her."

"Your aunt must have been a really good teacher, B. You made at least fifty outfits for my dolls! I'll never forget the elegant blue satin ball gown you created for my Madame Alexander."

B clicked her tongue, and in a strangely cocky manner responded, "Better than those from Lowenstein's?"

"Much better!"

My mother beamed.

"Momma, I'm having fun."

"And I thought you'd be bored. After all, Milam, you are a teenager."

"Oh no, in fact, I'd like to come back some day."

My grandmother smiled approvingly at me.

Writer, Writer

As we pulled into our driveway, Momma said, "Butch, I have another surprise."

"Oh dear," responded an anxious B. "Does it involve your car?"

"No, I've prepared your favorite pie. Lemon ice box. Who wants a piece?"

"I do, I do."

We gobbled the pie saving one small piece for Daddy, who was working late.

"Delicious, Mary Catherine, your meringue is perfect."

"Thanks, Butch. I'm glad you liked it. We had a nice time today."

"Yes, we did."

Were I able to step back in time, I would have gone inside that flower shop on Charlotte Street. I would have encouraged my grandmother to go with me and asked her a million questions about her years with Aunt Mamie. How rich would my future stories have been! Maybe my imagination would not have had to play such a central role in B's story. On our trip, my mother, who was a dedicated gardener, planted her own seeds for my first book, *A Flower Blooms on Charlotte Street*.

I would return to Asheville in 1983 with our three young children for a summer excursion.

The next time I visited was in the mid-nineties to do research for my book. Jamey and I walked into the railroad depot where we deduced my grandmother likely arrived. I stood on the tile floor wishing I could know for certain.

"Were you here, B? Was this where your Asheville adventure began?"

From an open window, came a gentle breeze. I took it as her "yes."

Aunt Mamie's house, a victim of the expressway, was long gone. However, there was a service station on the site. A few years later, the owner displayed *Charlotte Street* in his window.

My mother would keep herself in check for three and a half years, as long as she could. She relapsed when my father was transferred to Birmingham, and I was accepted at the University of Alabama.

Momma was a diehard University of Tennessee fan and made no bones about it.

"This is your father's fault," she slurred. "To save money on in-state tuition, he's turned you into a traitor."

In late August, my parents moved me into the freshman dorm at Alabama. I seem to recall Momma wearing something orange and white, UT's colors. She

Writer, Writer

never again set foot on the Tuscaloosa campus, not until 1967 for my graduation.

Vietnam

In October of 1967, a few short weeks after our sweet wedding, my bridegroom departed for a twelve-month tour of duty in Vietnam. His parents and I said our tearful goodbyes to Jamey at the Birmingham airport. After we attempted to choke down a lunch none of us could stomach, Mary and Ed Propst, shaking and filled with anxiety, returned to their home in Clanton, Alabama.

Alone at my parent's house, I crumbled into a million pieces. Four days later, I drove to Memphis to seek B's comfort. On a warm October afternoon, she and I sat on the front porch of her apartment. I was beyond miserable.

"A whole year, B. That's longer than forever."

My grandmother tried to convince me Jamey might return quickly.

"Don't you remember, Milam? Just after you two graduated, that Arab-Israeli conflict started and ended in the blink of an eye."

"I remember," I replied flatly.

"Little darling, it's even referred to as the *Six-Day War*."

I clung to B's hopeful thought for the first few months Jamey was in Vietnam.

Writer, Writer

The practical person she was, my grandmother also urged me to keep busy while my husband was overseas. I listened to her advice and landed a job at *The Birmingham News*. Once again the balm of writing would nurture me as it had throughout high school and college. I wrote to B every week including a clipping of every story with my new byline: Milam McGraw Propst.

In June, Jamey and I celebrated our first wedding anniversary with an R&R in Hawaii. When Jamey stepped off the airplane, the whole world came alive for me.

We walked hand in hand on the beach taking photos of swaying palm trees and crashing surf, of exquisite tropical flowers, and of Diamond Head. But mostly, we took photos of one another.

We drove our rental car up into the mountains and laughed as island winds whipped through our hair.

We enjoyed romantic dinners and drank in magnificent sunsets. After more than eight months apart, it was the "we" that made the difference.

As magical as was our time together, the upcoming farewell at week's end loomed large. I tried to push my anxious thoughts aside, but each picture perfect day melted away far too quickly. I took Jamey to his flight and boarded my plane back to Alabama.

"We" over, I was back to myself. Alone.

Upon my return to *The Birmingham News*, Martha Hood, the Women's Editor, coaxed me back from despair by assigning an article on our R&R. As always, writing provided solace. I hummed Don Ho's "Tiny Bubbles," wrote the feature, and started counting the days until the first week of October. July, August, and September inched along in slow motion.

"Done!" I crossed October 7 off the calendar with a triumphant red X.

My father honked the car horn. I took one last look in the mirror and sprinted out the front door.

"Ready to go to the airport, Honey?"

"Yes, I can't believe this is finally over."

Daddy dropped me at the terminal's front entrance and went to park. I saw Jamey's parents and rushed to greet them.

"Have you been here long?"

"Only a couple of hours," laughed Ed as he squeezed Mary's hand.

We embraced even tighter than on that agonizing day twelve months before. With their son far away, our frequent visits had forged a unique bond between Jamey's parents and me.

My heart rose in my throat when the airplane taxied into place.

Writer, Writer

"There he is!"

"You two, go to your boy."

I'll never forget the image of Jamey's parents running toward him with their welcoming arms waving wildly in unadulterated ecstasy.

"My baby boy!" exclaimed Mary.

My father had tears in his eyes, too. Was he remembering his own homecoming in 1945? Was he sad, because our time together was coming to an end? I believe Daddy was overcome, because his daughter's new life was finally beginning.

The following weekend, Mary and Ed's neighbors treated us to a "Welcome Home" barbeque in their backyard. The night of the party, it seemed as if all of Clanton turned out to salute Lt. Propst.

Naturally, he and I took a trip to Memphis. To our surprise, my grandmother had planned a festive dinner for us at the Knickerbocker Restaurant on Poplar Avenue. My entire family, all of whom had attended our wedding, applauded as we entered the private dining room.

After dinner as dishes were being cleared away, B rose from her seat.

"Thank you for coming to my little celebration for Lt. and Mrs. James Propst."

She reached in her purse and retrieved a small box.

"I suppose you're officially my grandson now," she began, "and I couldn't be prouder of you for serving our country."

Feeling somewhat ill at ease, Jamey thanked her.

"You best keep my granddaughter happy."

Everyone was laughing, but my grandmother meant exactly what she said. B then opened the box.

"Now it's my honor to present you with a small token of our appreciation for your service. Welcome home, young man."

With those words, she gave Jamey the Key to the City of Memphis.

Jamey was somewhat taken aback, but he was proud, too. "Thank you, B. How on earth did you accomplish this?"

"I have connections," she said lowering her eyes and smiling to herself.

Writer, Writer

Springfield and Beyond

After a month long leave, Jamey and I drove to Springfield, Massachusetts, where he was assigned to an Army induction center. His new workmates were military-minded and conservative. Mine were not. I'd found a job as a reporter for *The Springfield Daily News*. My co-workers were liberal and artistic.

We hosted several spirited social gatherings in our apartment. It was the height of the Vietnam conflict, so everyone's emotions ran raw. Our guests were either passionate pacifists or deep-rooted war hawks. There was no middle ground. Fortunately, the police only had to come once.

While at the newspaper, I was able to expand my writing skills and stretch my creative muscles. I also earned my one and only front page byline. The article chronicled our harrowing twenty-four hour bus ride from New York City to Springfield in the middle of a Nor'easter snowstorm.

My report included accolades to the West Point Glee Club. In a scene reminiscent of the epic film *Doctor Zhivago*, the young gray-caped gentlemen marched through thigh deep snow, all the time singing with bravado, as they moved two jack-knifed tractor trailer trucks out of our path.

Writer, Writer

My equally intrepid bridegroom and several of our fellow
passengers joined in their operation.

My file of stories was building by leaps and bounds.

After Jamey's military career came to an end, we
returned to Birmingham to settle into becoming ordinary
people with jobs, a first house, and, glory be, babies, three
of them, Amanda, William, and Jay. An only child, one
who babysat but once, I had zero experience with children.
Suffice to say, there was little room for writing. I had no
time to brush my teeth! However, I was too euphoric about
being a mother to care about anything but my family.

Too content to create? Perhaps. Even so, seeds like
tiny acorns were taking root. Once our children were in
school, I wrote freelance articles for magazines. Every now
and again, another root would shoot out and grab a rich bite
of soil.

Harry

Harry Chapin was a great songwriter, a humanitarian, an entertainer, and a tremendous storyteller. I saw him first on the Merv Griffin Show and discovered he was coming to Birmingham. I immediately ordered tickets. From then on, any time Harry came to town, Jamey and I were in his audience. Like the avid fans who adore Elvis, I swooned whenever the talented man walked on stage. I still play his music.

As mesmerized as I was by the entertainer himself, I was even more spellbound by Harry's interesting anecdotes. Upon leaving his concert for what was to be the last time, I turned to my husband.

"I enjoy telling stories, too. One of these days, Jamey Propst, I'm going to write a book."

July 16, 1981, Harry Chapin was killed in a horrific automobile accident in New York City. I reacted to his death as I would have that of a friend.

The following spring, we moved to Atlanta where I continued to embrace my chosen roll as a wife and mother. Little did I know my fascination with the songwriter was part of God's plan for my future.

Writer, Writer

Milam McGraw Propst

Empty Nest

My serious quest to become an author began in 1991. A volunteer throughout the years our children were in school, I was completely unprepared for them to go away to college. To my utter dismay, there was no PTA work awaiting me at The College of Charleston, Washington & Lee University, or the University of Georgia.

I had a full time job in public relations, but working only filled my days. In order to keep myself occupied, I signed up for a non-credit writing class at Oglethorpe University. The first night of class, I eyed the buildings before me. The architecture of Oglethorpe has the look of a medieval fortress. A few blocks from our house, the campus seemed to be in another country.

Our classroom had a high ceiling with floor length windows which provided a view of a neatly trimmed grass quadrangle. The academic aromas of chalk, old textbooks, and pencil sharpenings smelled familiar. Almost expecting Mr. Scarrit to appear, I felt at home in a space as aesthetically appealing as Woods Hall.

Our instructor, Carol Lee Lorenzo, is a recipient of the Flannery O'Connor Award for Short Fiction. A suitable environment plus a fine teacher, the stars were lining up for me. Eight of us, a mixture of men and women, old and older, gathered around a large rectangular table.

Writer, Writer

Carol Lee began by explaining the purpose of our six-week course. "If anyone among you is here either to get published or to make significant money, you'd better leave."

She warned the group that only six-tenths of one percent of people who write books will be published. I studied the disappointed faces of those around me. The instructor continued, "If you are here because you love to write, please stay."

We eight kept our seats.

As I drove home, I made up my mind not to concern myself with achieving any specific goal. I pulled into the garage and turned off the car. I decided, then and there, fiction would become my field. At best, I would get a book published. At least, my writing would become a pleasant hobby allowing me to get my mind off missing Amanda, William, and Jay.

Jamey had played golf for more than thirty years. Thus far, he'd won a silver brandy snifter, a couple of shirts, and some golf equipment. The only monetary reward for his considerable efforts had come from an occasional wager made with his foursome on Saturday mornings. Along similar lines, creative writing would become my amateur sport.

I crafted short stories for children and found the work fulfilling. Under Carol Lee's guidance, our class progressed rapidly during the six weeks. So enthusiastic were we, the same group signed up again and again for the next two years. Carol Lee, who has a background in theater, would read our work aloud. She breathed life into our stories. I'll never forget the first time I heard the voice of my main character, my grandmother, Ociee Nash.

"But, Papa, if I hold my chin up," read Carol Lee, "tears will run down my face and ruin my dress."

Carol Lee had tears in her own eyes. Others in our class were crying, too. Was my writing that dreadful?

"Where did this come from?" asked Carol Lee.

"William's foot," I stuttered.

"His foot?"

William had suffered a terrible injury in September of his junior year at W&L. I had just gotten home from the office when our telephone rang.

"Are you the mother of William Propst?" said the voice on the other end.

"Yes, I am."

"This is Doctor Dick at Stonewall Jackson Hospital," the voice continued. "Your son has turned his foot around backwards."

"Okay, which member of Phi Delta Theta is this?" I snapped. "I don't think you're very funny."

"Mrs. Propst, I'm afraid this is no joke."

Writer, Writer

Jamey drove into our garage; and I raced to his arms, frantically, tearfully telling him about William. Within ten minutes of the surgeon's call, I was headed to Virginia with a change or two of clothes, a pair of pajamas, a credit card, a toothbrush, and a yellow legal pad and pen. Driving well into the night, I prayed every mile of the frenzied journey.

Dr. Dick's grim prognosis repeated itself over and over.

"Freak accident. Skateboard. Achilles tendon. He may have trouble walking."

Walking? Our son was a gifted athlete. He'd excelled in soccer and football at Marist High School. He played wide receiver for the W&L Generals. William was a beautiful runner. And fast. Very fast.

I made it to the hospital a couple of hours before his surgery. Our handsome son was lying in a cold hospital bed. He was obviously in excruciating pain; but like the macho guy he has always been, William managed a faint smile.

I choked back tears as some now blurred memory of a medical person wheeled my boy down a long sterile hallway. William disappeared into an operating room. The doors swung shut.

Our son's traumatic injury would change the entire focus of my simple children's story. No longer was I going to create a charming picture book about my grandmother, a little girl named Ociee, who rode on a train to North Carolina. The story would include the anguish of a distressed nine-year-old child saying farewell to the only family she had ever known.

As William slept fitfully during his three-day hospital stay, I scribbled random notes on a legal pad. Once home in Atlanta, the despair I was feeling about our son spilled onto paper. William's accident, along with my own childhood memories, continued to come forth to serve me in my work.

Page forty-nine in *A Flower Blooms on Charlotte Street* tells the story of Ociee's tearful farewell to her father and brothers. I cry whenever I reread it. I also cry when I watch the movie version of the book as actress Skyler Day, beats on the train's window mouthing, "Papa, Papa."

I'm welling up with tears as I write these words. I cry for my grandmother. I cry for the pain William endured his junior year of college.

The morning of his operation, I was sitting alone in the surgical waiting area, alternately shaking and praying. A beautiful young woman appeared with flowers and a book of poetry. She was wearing a brown suede skirt and leather boots.

"Hi, I'm Abigail Kane. I'm a friend of your son."

We sat together.

Finally, Dr. Dick walked into the room. We sprang to our feet.

"We got real lucky," he announced. "The tendon snapped back into place. William has a metal plate to secure his ankle. It's going to take a while, but your son will be all right."

"Thank the Lord!"

I exhaled for the first time since Dr. Dick's phone call. I hugged the surgeon. I hugged Abigail, and she hugged me.

Throughout William's lengthy recovery, he got to know Abigail better. She was one of the numerous volunteers, who drove him around campus helping with his books as he navigated on clumsy crutches.

Mercifully, William recovered so well, he was able to return for his senior year of football. Jamey and I attended every game in his 1994 season, and so did Abigail. They married in 1999 and are the proud parents of our remarkable grandsons, Loftin and Emmett. From William's unthinkable accident came his wife, his sons, and my first efforts toward becoming an author.

Ninety Percent Persistence

Carole Lee's class was a gift for me, for the eight of us. Those Monday nights were as refreshing as an ice cold drink of fresh squeezed lemonade on a thirsty August afternoon. As our confidence grew, several of us began to submit work to publishers.

Moving at full speed writing the Ociee Nash story, I hoped our children would enjoy reading something based on their great grandmother, and learn more about their Southern heritage and the South as it existed a century ago.

Their reactions were mixed ranging from "Uh huh" to "Go for it, Mom."

In the back of my optimistic mind lurked the idea that maybe, just maybe, someone might be interested in publishing my work. As Carol Lee stressed, "Ten percent talent, ninety percent persistence."

Her words carried me.

The first time I heard Marc Jolley's name, I was visiting my family in Memphis. My book finished, I had been unsuccessful in finding a publisher and was working on other projects. I'd submitted numerous query letters to publishing houses and literary agents. I'd acquired a voluminous heap of rejection slips from New York to California. Fortunately, I did receive a few positive notes; but mostly those bursts of encouragement were trumped by a significant number of standard postcards stating, "Thanks, but we suggest you find another publishing house."

A literary agent in California replied in a particularly insulting manner. Mr. Levin returned my own query letter to me. My own letter! On said letter, in pencil not in pen, the insensitive jerk scribbled the four-letter word "pass."

I was beyond furious. An experienced rejection slip receiver, Mr. Levin's "pass" was a kick in my stomach. Pencil. My own letter. I was tempted to write back saying, "Wow, I passed! Thank you, Mr. Levin. What's our next step?"

The only thing keeping me from responding in kind was my fear the West Coast clod would subsequently judge every Southern writer by me, a glowing example of naiveté.

Carol Lee's advice and my innate optimism would triumph, and I continued to pursue my quixotic quest. Throughout 1996, following the current publishing guidelines, I would mail one query letter at a time with an SASE, self-addressed stamped envelope. I'd always have another package ready to send.

My beloved grandmother B had passed away just after my fortieth birthday. I will miss her for as long as I remain on earth. Anytime I'm in Memphis, I go by Calvary Cemetery and sit beside her grave.

Ociee Nash Whitman, November 8, 1889 – February 14, 1985

During one visit, I traced her name in the letters of her tombstone. That's Ociee with two e's.

At the suggestion of my classmates at Oglethorpe, I'd taken the second "e" off her name to make it easier for young readers to pronounce. I spell-checked and erased every extra "e." My book's hero, my darling B became "Ocie." Immediately, I realized I'd sinned.

She had added the "e" herself and liked becoming Ociee. She thought it sounded less rural, more refined, and certainly sophisticated. Christened Josephine Elizabeth Nash, her nickname was supposed to be "Josie,' but her brother Ben couldn't pronounce j's. Soon everyone in the Nash family was calling her Osie, then Ocie.

Kneeling by her headstone, I confessed my grievous sin to B; and I shared my hopes of finding a publisher. I leaned closer to her grave and whispered an even more outlandish thought.

"B, one of these days there's going to be a movie about your story."

Arriving back at Daddy's house, I was told Jamey phoned saying a publisher from Mercer University Press was trying to get in touch with me.

Writer, Writer

"Here's his number," said Daddy excitedly waving a piece of paper, "A Dr. Jolley said to call at your convenience."

"My convenience!"

Without putting down my purse, I dialed his number. After all, hadn't Ociee Nash, a take-charge person, just selected the publisher of her choice?

"Hello, Dr. Jolley, this is Milam Propst."

I assume we had some cordial dialogue before I asked the question which was smoldering in my brain. Knowing how I behave, maybe not. I blurted out, "Dr. Jolley, would it be okay to spell my character's name O-c-i-e-E?"

Somewhat perplexed, the publisher recommended I spell her name correctly. Halleluiah, I'd gone to confession, received absolution, and the damage would be repaired!

I'd also gotten way ahead of myself.

He sighed and gently explained, "Mrs. Propst, although I am personally drawn to your story, I'm afraid Mercer does not publish fiction."

I crumbled.

Sensing my disappointment, he added, "I believe in your story and look forward to the day I can read it to my young son, Patrick."

Uncharacteristically brazen of me, I asked Dr. Jolley about other publishers who might consider my book.

He generously gave me a few names and offered to stay in touch. For months, I sent out queries dropping the name of Dr. Marc Jolley, Mercer University Press.

Dreaded rejections kept coming.

Late on a Friday afternoon, our phone rang.

"Milam, this is Marc. Any luck yet?"

"Hi, Marc. Sadly, no," I answered. Attempting to sound upbeat, I laughed nervously. "But I'm not about to quit."

"Mercer has had a good year," he said. "We're going to take a chance on a work of fiction."

My heart pounded louder than a base drum.

"I've suggested yours."

"What?"

"We're going to offer you a contact for a 'to be named' story about Ociee Nash. That's Ociee with two e's!"

The rest of the conversation remains a blur. I remember thanking Marc a million times. Finally, I let the man hang up. I hugged our dog, Nestle, and burst into tears. She understood, having been at my side for every word I typed.

There were no cell phones then. I was tethered to the kitchen wall phone by a long extension cord. Like a rubber ball on a wooden paddle, I bounced back and forth as I called Jamey at the bank.

Writer, Writer

"Guess what?" I screamed. "Mercer University Press is going to publish Ociee!"

Silence.

"Did you hear me?"

"I'm dumbstruck, Baby Doll," he replied. "I'm proud of you."

"I'm proud of me, too."

It must be explained Jamey is realistic, almost to the point of being a pessimist. He was acting characteristically honest when he commented, "I never thought you'd get that thing published."

"I know. You call me *Don Quixote*."

"Tell you what, Baby Doll. This is one damn big windmill."

The second person I contacted was Jay. A student at the University of Georgia, I was shocked to reach him on the first try. As most parents know, college kids can be elusive creatures.

Jay contributed the last line of my book. Home visiting for the weekend, he was in the basement practicing on his guitar. I was upstairs stuck with how to end the story. Frustrated, I stood up, stretched, and printed out the last page, short the one sentence.

He was sitting on the side of his bed. "What's up, Mom?"

I asked our son, a musician and songwriter, for his thoughts. I read the passage and described the message I wanted to convey.

He replied, "Keep it simple, Mom. How about 'A moment later, she was gone.'"

His words conclude the novel, beautifully.

"Jay! Guess what? I have glorious news!"

Writer, Writer

Books, Books, Books!

The UPS man rang the doorbell. Alarmed, Nestle went berserk. When I spotted Mercer's logo, I did, too.

"They're here; they're here at last!"

With his eyes fixed on Nestle and on me, the delivery man quickly placed two large boxes in the entry hall.

"Thank you, thank you, THANK YOU!" I squealed, embracing the uneasy man.

Apprehensive about his customer and her big dog, the poor guy sprinted to his truck. Laughing at him, I ripped open the shipping carton and tore away the packing materials. I saw *A Flower Blooms on Charlotte Street* for the very first time and cradled a copy as if it were a newborn infant.

"Oh, my heart."

"By Milam McGraw Propst." My byline.

The cover is a pleasing watercolor painted by Macon artist, Barclay Burns. It depicts Aunt Mamie's front porch in Asheville. Readers have said they keep the book in their guest rooms because of its gorgeous cover.

Mercer thoughtfully presented me with the original painting. It hangs in our dining room as a reminder of how fortunate I am. Alongside *Charlotte Street* hangs an equally

Writer, Writer

appealing Barclay Burns watercolor, one Mercer commissioned for the sequel, *Ociee on Her Own*. The talented team of Mary Frances and Jim Burt designed *Charlotte Street*'s cover and those for my next two novels.

Our daughter Amanda had taken a picture of me for the back cover. My stance is a sassy one with my head cocked with my hands on my hips. I was trying to encourage Nestle to pose with me, but the old pup shyly refused the spotlight, and Amanda snapped the shot.

I was admiring the cover when Jamey arrived home.

"Hey, Baby Doll. Whoa! Is this your book?"

"Sure is," I said smugly.

"Are you pleased?"

"I don't know. I'm too nervous to look inside. Will you?"

"Will I what?"

"Look inside. What if there aren't any words? What if the whole publishing thing is a figment of my crazy imagination?"

"Speaking of *crazy*," said Jamey shaking his head.

"I suppose you're right."

I gathered my courage.

"There are words, Jamey, lots of 'em!"

He suggested we go out to celebrate. We went to our favorite Mexican spot, Taxco. I picked up a copy of the book as we were leaving. Not prudent. We ordered cheese dip, but I hardly ate a bite. I was worried cheese would drip off a chip and ruin the cover. Clearly, I needed to calm down.

The Brantleys and the Winstons hosted a marvelous book release party for *Charlotte Street*. Everyone made me feel so special that April afternoon. My sole regret was not publicly thanking Mary and Marvin, Marilynn and Ron; but I was too bashful to call attention to myself.

A few weeks later at Ave Bransford's party, I suffered from the same shyness. I sat quietly signing books as guests milled around eating goodies and chatting. Their voices echoing around me, I summoned my courage.

"Ahem, ladies, your attention, please."

I flushed as their faces turned toward me.

"Ave, I want to thank you and the other ladies for hosting this lovely party for Ociee Nash and me. My grandmother and I have small tokens of appreciation for you."

I handed each hostess a bottle of lavender hand lotion explaining the scent was my grandmother's favorite.

One of the guests commented, "So Ociee Nash was a real person!"

"Yes, indeed." I talked for twenty minutes.

Writer, Writer

I share this story with students when they complain about being nervous when talking in front of groups.

"I'm living proof that even a grown person can master a new skill. The trick is simple. Pick a topic which captures your interest so much you want to share it with an audience."

I'll always remain grateful to the many generous people who hosted book signings for me. One gathering was held at The Norcross Station Café, which is a converted railroad depot with trains regularly rumbling by. During the party, with each train, my young friend Dana, her mother Dannie, and their group of guests joyfully shouted, "Hello, Ociee! Goodbye, Ociee!"

.Another event was a reception at St. Agnes Academy, the Catholic girls' school where I'd earned my first byline. The alumni director, Jane Tonning, organized an afternoon tea party in the front lobby of my former school. I had not walked through those doors in forty years; yet the open arms of teachers and staff greeted me with the same warmth as had the principal, Sister Suzanne, in the fall of 1951.

I stood, microphone in hand, gazing into a group of friendly faces. I addressed my beaming father and his guests, my cousins and former classmates, and old friends, including my childhood pal, Margaret, and the Harrison family. Another lifelong friend, Betty Ann, and her daughter, Emily, had traveled from Arkansas to share the unique afternoon with us.

Several St. Agnes alumnae, long deceased, were also by my side. Included were my mother, my grandmother, my Godmother Tillie Borg, and our family's treasure, Ann Whitman. Because of our strong family ties, Momma, B, Tillie, and Ann are always but a whisper away from me.

I couldn't have known on that June day more than a decade ago; but in January, 2011, Ociee Nash Whitman, Class of 1908, would be inducted into the prestigious St. Agnes Academy Hall of Fame. I proudly accepted a beautifully engraved crystal vase in her honor.

Writer, Writer

PR Man

"Let's drop by Barnes & Noble," said Jamey.

"Why?"

"Play along with me. This will be fun."

It's pointless trying to stop my husband when he's on a mission. We walked in the side door of the bookstore.

Jamey whispered, "Go hide behind the magazines."

"Hide?"

"Shhhh, just do it."

With me out of sight, the Man of My Dreams went up to the checkout counter and bellowed, "I'm looking for a new book by a local author. Let's see, I forget her name, oh yes, it's Propst. P-r-o-p-s-t."

His voice grew louder with every letter.

Jamey all but shouted, "Her name is Milam Propst.

I think the title is *A Flower Blooms on Charlotte Street*."

Raising his voice so any shopper within a mile might hear, he announced, "I understand it's a great book."

People were watching, lots of people. Jamey had captured his audience. He could be a marketing mastermind if only he cared as much about other people's products.

The clerk looked on her computer.

"Yes, sir, we have the book. I'll have someone get it for you while you pay."

Writer, Writer

Jamey opened his wallet and turned five shades of red. He put his hand behind his back and motioned for me to come out of hiding. Sheepishly, I walked toward the counter.

"What?"

"Do you have your credit card?"

I dug in my purse. "Yes." I slipped it into his hand.

Placing the book in a bag the clerk said, "Thank you, Mr. Propst. It's nice to meet you, Mrs. Propst."

En route for her second knee replacement, my friend Georganne insisted her husband stop to purchase a copy of my book.

"Didn't you have other things on your mind?" I asked. "Major surgery for example!"

"Well, yes, but I needed something good to read in the hospital."

Georganne's surgery was a success, but she would remain housebound for days. As is customary, people brought meals. When I entered with mine, I found the darling lady seated in her kitchen.

"Good for you; I figured you'd be in bed."

"You know me better than that."

A Cheshire cat's grin lighted her face.

"What's your big smile about?"

Before she could answer, her husband Bob walked by.

"Did you tell Milam?"

"Tell me what? Wait, you two have another grandchild on the way!"

"Nope," Georganne replied. Her dimples deepened.

"So what's your big secret?"

She ran her fingers through her blond bangs brushing them back from her forehead. "I found her."

"Found who?"

"Your teacher, Sister Thomas Margaret. That's who."

"Georganne, she's been missing for decades. Nobody knows her whereabouts."

"I do. Here's her address."

Totally stunned, I asked how my friend managed to solve a mystery even the people at St. Pius couldn't.

"While I was recuperating, I had nothing better to do with my time. I did some research."

I sent the nun a copy of *Charlotte Street*. As on the novel's acknowledgement page, I penned long overdue words of gratitude for the important role the exceptional English teacher had played in my journalism career.

She sent back a chapter by chapter critique some eighteen pages long and concluded her correspondence writing, "Sometimes, old English teachers come back to

Writer, Writer

haunt their students. This time the student has come back to haunt the old English teacher."

The Interview

With *Charlotte Street* thriving, I got back to work on another book. When Mercer published *It May Not Leave a Scar*, it turned out to be an entirely different experience for me.

Dripping wet and uninspired, I stood staring aimlessly into my closet.

The clock flashed 2:45---2:46---2:47. Andrea, a reporter from *The Sandy Springs Neighbor,* was scheduled to arrive any minute.

Was that a car? Oh no, what would I do! I clutched the towel and peeked out the window. The car continued up Cherrywood Lane.

A reprieve.

I continued to rifle through plastic coat hangers draped with unsuitable, out of style, ill-fitting clothing. I admired my pedicure. Andrea's photographer could take her picture of my feet.

"Hello, closet. After this interview, I'm driving your contents to Goodwill."

With every dress, blouse, skirt, and pair of pants purged, I'd begin anew with the help of Abigail, my fashion-forward daughter-in-law.

2:56. Digital clocks are entirely too accurate for my taste.

Writer, Writer

I grabbed my funky blue dress with its gorgeous hand-painted jacket. An artsy, fartsy garment can go almost anywhere and be appropriate, especially if one is an author. *Author*, how I relished my title! I'd purchased the outfit because the soothing shades of blue and green complemented so nicely the cover of *Charlotte Street*. I slipped the dress over my head. Eh gads! It was too tight.

I reached for my trusty black skirt, always flattering. Until 2:59. I tugged frantically at the zipper. Our evil dry cleaner shrank my blue dress and the skirt. Had she done so on purpose? I should have given the woman a book.

"Look at youself, Milam. If I didn't know better, I'd swear you were eight months pregnant."

I tried futilely to suck in and zip up. No go. I stepped out of the skirt trying to avoid viewing myself from a sideways angle. I vowed to begin a diet Monday. The weight gain wasn't entirely my fault. With every booksigning at a Barnes & Noble, came a box of Godiva chocolates. I had to be polite, right? Every yummy bite found a new home around my middle.

The clock clicked 3:00. I jerked a long floral skirt from its hanger. It zipped! Fretfully buttoning a green silk blouse, I slid into black sandals and admired my rose-colored toenails.

The doorbell rang.

"BRRROOUFF!" As usual, Nestle took off as if she'd been fired from a circus cannon. Her toenails clicking on the waxed floor, eighty-six pounds of snarling German shepherd-golden retriever bounded around the corner. As with the UPS man, Nestle deemed any person at our front door her enemy. The dog continued to growl and snort while I fumbled with the key.

I held a death grip on her collar and opened the door.

"I'm Andrea from *The Neighbor*."

The attractive young reporter smiled tentatively. She was dressed in business causal, while I was apparently en route to a luau.

"Nestle won't hurt you. She's all bark, no bite."

On cue, the dog snarled bearing her long teeth, her wolf ancestry evident.

Andrea motioned for the photographer. "We'll take your picture first. Then I'll do the interview."

The interview. My stomach tightened.

After a couple of shots in my office, we walked outside to the garden. Nestle, finally accepting the newspaper people, posed with me.

When the article appeared, our neighbor Wylda remarked, "Congratulations, Milam. We noticed Nestle was smiling as proudly as you."

Writer, Writer

It May Not Leave a Scar had been released three days prior. I was prepared. The night before, I'd gone over everything I would and would not discuss. So why I was in such turmoil?

Andrea and I made ourselves comfortable in the sunroom.

I tend to come up with improbable goals. My latest aspiration was to save my big revelation for a future appearance on *The Oprah Winfrey Show.* I had no intention of giving Andrea the scoop. I planned to share my earth shattering announcement with Oprah herself and had rehearsed the scene a hundred times. There I was on Oprah's stage seated in her special guest chair. The front row would be filled with family, friends, and the folks from Mercer Press. The audience was packed with people, all of whom had devoured *Scar*. Oprah would ask me penetrating questions. Finally, she would lean forward, look me square in the eye, and exclaim, "Milam, your book is NOT a work of fiction, am I right?"

On national television, in front of millions of viewers, I would hesitate, but only for dramatic effect, ever building to a higher level of suspense. Finally, I would exclaim, "Oprah, you are absolutely correct!"

Applauding and cheering, the audience would rise to its feet. My friends would be weeping, while my family cheered wildly. Fans of the book would nod knowingly. I would have put a new face on the image of the dysfunctional family. My experience would bring encouragement to legions of broken spirits.

My first words to the reporter from *The Sandy Springs Neighbor* were, "Andrea, do you want to know the truth?"

I made the right decision. Oprah's people never called.

Writer, Writer

Why Not Laugh?

Writing *Scar* was a catharsis for me. I started the book in July, 1996, just after my mother turned eighty-three. Momma had been sober since she was eighty-one or so. Exactly when she stopped drinking isn't clear in my mind. Because her sobriety seemed too good to be true, I wouldn't allow myself to trust her for months. I was waiting for the second shoe to drop.

My father had divorced my mother on their fiftieth wedding anniversary. In our family, drama was an art form. With Daddy out of the picture, Momma had become my complete responsibility. Writers write, especially stressed out writers like me. Another book was inevitable.

I wrote *Scar* as a fictional account, a book meant to encourage myself and others to forgive. As the years went by, however, I yearned to revisit those pages, but with an entirely different point of view. In *Writer, Writer*, I decided to draw attention to another side of my mother's story. The comedy.

One morning Momma got up, called *The Birmingham News*, and placed an ad offering her automobile for sale. A man called right away. He purchased my mother's car, drove down her street, turned right, and robbed the local branch bank.

Writer, Writer

A fast thinking bystander jotted down the tag number. Moments later the usual quiet of Momma's neighborhood was disrupted when a police squad car, its blue lights flashing, flew up Heritage Circle. According to my mother's next door neighbor, two officers jumped from their squad car, and, with weapons drawn, charged up the McGraw's driveway.

Amazingly, Momma came to the door. As a rule, she did not allow anything to interrupt *General Hospital*. The sirens may have sparked her interest.

"Are you the owner of a tan 1979 Chevrolet?"

"It is none of your damn beeswax," she slurred.

"Are you Mrs. Mary Catherine McGraw?"

"Who ELSE would I be?"

"Ma'am, do you know where your vehicle, the Chevrolet, is?"

"How the hell would I know? I sold the damn thing this morning."

"Mrs. McGraw, your vehicle was involved in a bank robbery."

"For Gawd's sake, do I look like somebody who'd stick up a bank?"

"No, ma'am. You don't."

"Now, don't worry about a thing, Mrs. McGraw. We'll take care of this for you."

"You damn well better! You're making me miss my program."

"Sorry for the trouble, Mrs. McGraw."

The officers tipped their caps, exchanged a couple of pleasantries, and quickly exited Momma's home. She called me as soon as her soap opera took a commercial break.

"Some damn fool cops have been here."

"Good grief, Momma! Why?"

Not that wacky telephone calls from and about my mother were uncommon, but this one took the cake. I listened to my mother as a knot started burning a brand new hole in my stomach.

"I asked those idiots, 'Do I look like someone who would stick up a bank?'"

My mother loved her detective magazines and watched every police show on television, her favorite being *Dragnet* starring Jack Webb as Detective Joe Friday. It would be only natural for Momma to use lingo like "stick up."

"One of the cops insinuated he'd been to our house before," Momma continued, muttering under her breath.

I could believe that. The local firefighters had also made numerous visits to Heritage Circle. Momma was a chain smoker and somewhat slipshod when it came to extinguishing her cigarette butts. Once sober and back to behaving as her properly raised polite self, my grateful mother would take a homemade lemon meringue pie by the fire station. A Southern lady, Mrs. McGraw was consistent in thanking the nice gentlemen for putting out every single one of her numerous fires. The local furniture store also appreciated my mother's steady business.

"I told the fool cop he was sadly mistaken."

"Good for you, Momma."

"Humph, I'm a law abiding citizen."

The knot in my stomach dissolved. A good laugh always provided relief along with material for stories.

The next crisis is chronicled in *It May Not Leave a Scar*. In a nutshell, my mother suffered a terrible fall; again the neighbors contacted me. Following an emergency hip replacement, we moved her to Atlanta. As things were heating up for us, I suppose life calmed down for the police officers and firemen who serve Momma's former Crestline community. I wonder if they miss the excitement. I'm quite sure the firefighters yearn for her lemon pies.

Living in Atlanta, my mother had three options for doing errands. She could call a taxi cab, ride in the retirement home van, or engage me. Her new routine moved along smoothly until telephone customers throughout the Atlanta area were mandated to use an area code, even when calling next door.

"For Gawd's sake, Milam, this is the most ridiculous thing I've ever heard!"

"Progress, Momma."

"To hell with progress."

For the remainder of her life, unless it was a dire emergency, Momma adamantly refused to use her phone. On a positive note, she stopped calling cabs to take her to the liquor store. After more than six decades of renouncing the precepts of *Alcoholics Anonymous*, her aversion to dialing three extra numbers . . . sobriety.

Located on the front of an old fashioned telephone, the dial is a circular device with numbers zero through nine. God bless her, Momma never accepted anything she considered modern. Push button phones proved no exception.

"I can't see well enough to push those damn buttons."

No longer drinking vodka, Momma turned to chocolate ice cream to feed her demons. She picked up a gallon or two every Tuesday when the van provided trips to the grocery store. She consumed bowl after bowl of chocolate ice cream each week along with a half dozen Hershey almond bars. A couple of times, Momma ran out of chocolate; and I was summoned by phone. In my mother's view, having no chocolate qualified as an emergency.

"Don't forget, Milam. Get Hershey with nuts."

"Nuts," appropriate. We were a couple of nuts, my mother and I.

I could not have been happier Momma found an alternative to alcohol. The two of us were swimming our way back to one another in a sea of chocolate.

Upon learning my book's title, *It May Not Leave a Scar*, Jamey remarked, "It's okay, but I have a better idea."

"Uh hum."

"You could call it *Too Damn Old to Drink*."

I had to laugh.

Writing as Therapy

The first time I scribbled down this short piece, it was not meant for publication. I wrote it to work through Momma's visit to the office of our dentist and friend, Tom Carroll.

"Don't worry," assured Tom. "I can handle your mother."

The trouble started when his assistant asked Momma to fill out a new patient form. She was accustomed to being pampered by family doctors in Birmingham and Memphis, men she'd known for decades, old-fashioned physicians who require no paperwork.

"Uumph," she groused.

"Can I help, Momma?"

"Haven't you done enough already?" she growled.

Momma viewed any type of paperwork as an intrusion into her privacy. When she came to the line requiring information about her artificial hip, she left it blank.

"Mrs. McGraw, you may come back now."

Momma rose from her seat, frowned at me, and followed the dental assistant.

I waited nervously sipping coffee and whipping through the pages of a magazine. Articles about what? I was clueless. A write-up about an invasion from outer space or pictures of my own children would have gone

Writer, Writer

unnoticed. I struck up a conversation with the woman seated next to me. We enjoyed a genial chat about the cooling weather and upcoming holidays.

"My mother is going to eat Dr. Carroll for lunch."

Not making further eye contact, the patient gathered her purse and umbrella and moved quickly to the other side of the waiting room.

Tom cheerfully greeted his new patient. He was aware of my mother's hip replacement. I'd told him and everybody else in our church about her accident, surgery, and subsequent rehabilitation. She needed their prayers. I needed their pity.

Innocently, tactfully, Tom confronted Momma.

"I hope you're feeling well today, Mrs. McGraw. Hmmm, it seems we have an unanswered question here about your hip replacement."

"It's none of your damn business. Aren't you supposed to concern yourself with my TEETH?"

Patiently, the gentle doctor attempted to explain the situation.

"Dear lady, because I know you have prosthesis, I must insist you take antibiotics prior to having your teeth cleaned. It's our policy. My receptionist will be happy to reschedule another visit as soon as you like."

Momma sat in the dental chair glaring at Tom.

He smiled sweetly. "This is for your own protection, Mrs. McGraw. Any dental work, even a simple cleaning, could lead to an infection."

He paused adding firmly, "I don't want to alarm you, but you could very well experience serious problems. Mrs. McGraw, you want to avoid such a catastrophe, don't you?"

Momma pulled herself out of the chair, "What I want to avoid is you!"

My mother stormed out of Tom Carroll's office. As she blew past me, she puffed up like a dowager countess. "I am not pleased with your doctor friend."

My jaw dropped open. The other woman made a sign of the cross.

Momma flung open the door. "I am going outside for a cigarette. Join me, if you wish."

I apologized to Tom and to his staff.

"I'll say this, Milam. You certainly didn't exaggerate in the slightest about your mother!"

Momma found another dentist. The woman's practice required dental forms, but my mother never mentioned her hip to the unsuspecting doctor. She would pass away with all her teeth.

Writer, Writer

Tincture of Time

Momma's story had taken forever to reach the surface. Sometime in the late seventies, Jamey bought me a desk and typewriter.

"Baby Doll, I think you should write about your weird family."

My husband had the right idea, but I was a busy young mother nursing the small hurts of our children. I was also nursing my own deep wounds. It would be more than a decade before I gathered the courage to write about my mother's alcoholism.

A novella on the theme of forgiveness, its original title was *Are You in There, Momma?* The story began with a chilling flashback to my grandfather's suicide. I mailed a skeletal eighty-nine-page manuscript to Mercer and was midway through a rewrite when Marc phoned.

"I like your story, but you need to expand, adding more of the painful details."

"Why? The people, who choose to read it, know about alcoholism."

"If you're not forthcoming with your readers, they won't grasp your need to forgive your mother."

"Sorry, Marc. I just can't do it."

Writer, Writer

For the first time, he and I had arrived at an impasse. Marc wanted more than I could, would, or should reveal.

A few weeks later, I attended a luncheon and listened to a speech given by author, Wally Lamb. I called Marc the next morning.

"I've had an epiphany!"

"Really, tell me."

I thought I heard him yawn.

"I went to hear Wally Lamb speak."

"Milam, everyone, who hears Wally Lamb, has an epiphany."

"I'm going to write Momma's story as a work of fiction."

Marc was silent. Then he replied, "Brilliant."

In a work of fiction, Momma's character was free to take on a personality all her own. The reckless eighteen-year-old was no longer my mother. As I wrote her dialogue, it came not from Momma's tongue but from the lips of Imogene Sinclair. When she made inappropriate statements, I could chuckle. No longer her embarrassed daughter, I was an objective storyteller.

Harvey Clark, my father's fictional name, granted me the same flexibility. I wasn't tied to the image of the man I knew as Daddy, because I was writing about a person called Harvey.

I could also write from an author's viewpoint regarding B. Neither my grandmother nor Sarah Sinclair ever came to grips with her husband's suicide or with the alcoholism of their only child. I could compose Sarah's dialogue without my heart breaking in two.

Writing my book placed me squarely in the shoes of each character, but there was a negative aspect. As I empathized with my family, my guilt intensified. Were I to look at a photograph of Momma, Daddy, or B, their eyes would meet mine.

"Don't talk about the suicide with strangers," warned one.

"How could you say such awful things about your mother?" Another would condemn.

"Milam, it's our family's business," commented a third.

"I am so sorry," said one. Finally.

Even as fiction, the telling of the story awakened sleeping ghosts. These were not the imagined beings which inhabited the Hector house. These ghosts were real. As I wrote, I battled the specters of distant screams and ancient kitchen fires. I again heard the sound of bare feet stumbling in the night. I traveled back to witness battles between my parents and listened to weeping and foul words mumbled outside my bedroom door. As I wrote, I could smell vodka and the stale scent of cigarette ashes.

Marc plowed through the fictionalized manuscript and continued to demand even more. He asked Kevin Manus to join us on the project. Like Marc, Kevin urged me to paint increasingly vivid pictures. There was many a day I wanted to be like *Blondie* in the comic strips. As she chased *Dagwood* around the house with a rolling pin, I would have gladly taken the weapon to Kevin's head.

It was Christmas Eve night in 2000. Kevin and I were on the phone thrashing out yet another traumatic scene. In the background, his nieces and nephews sang *Joy to the World*. My own family, Jamey, Amanda, William, and Jay waited in the den to unwrap gifts. I prayed it would be worth all the angst.

Caught in the Act

Marc called me to describe what Mercer Press and the Burts were planning for the book's cover. A glossy white jacket with *It May Not Leave a Scar* would feature the photograph of an antique sterling silver whiskey flask. Across the flask would be placed a single pink rose.

"Perfect!" I said. "Momma loved roses. And she certainly loved vodka."

Earlier that day, Marc was seated at his desk waiting for the designers, Mary Frances and Jim, to come. He looked at his watch. They would be arriving any minute, so he retrieved the flask from his shopping bag.

Kevin stuck his head in the door and caught sight of the flask in Marc's hand.

"Oh no, Dr. Jolley, are things really that bad?"

Shy, quiet, and most certainly not a drinker, Marc was mortified.

An unlikely and priceless image, I laughed out loud when he shared his most embarrassing moment with me.

Writer, Writer

The Decree

Daddy flew over from Memphis for the weekend. His timing was good because Mercer had just sent the final proof pages for *Scar*. Knowing he would delight in becoming part of the process, I couldn't wait to show him.

My proud father had been a marketing goldmine for *Charlotte Street*. He'd rarely gone a month without ordering additional copies to give his friends, his doctors, people who worked at Kroger, his pharmacist, and the folks at his bank.

During our frequent phone conversations, I shared with him many details about my upcoming book.

"I think this is great, Honey," he said. "I'm glad you're finally getting things off your chest."

In all honesty, my father had more than a fondness for scotch. The afternoon I picked him up at the airport, it was evident he'd taken advantage of the free drinks in the first class section of the Delta jet. His inebriation had not worn off when we sat down to dinner.

"How's your book coming?"

"Pretty good, Daddy," I grinned. "I'll show you the proofs after we eat."

He took a bite of his steak. "I'm glad you and your mother are getting along better."

"Me, too."

He took a swallow of his scotch and water. "Sometimes I feel so damn guilty."

His comment took me completely by surprise. As a younger Milam, I would have spoken up to say I was doing perfectly fine with Momma, and to insist he shouldn't feel guilty. The older, healthier Milam sat quietly and cherished his apology.

Then, without any warning whatsoever, Daddy pounded his fist on the table and shouted, "Milam, I forbid you to publish the damn book!"

Bewildered beyond measure, everyone immediately stopped eating. Jamey choked on his last bite. I stared at my father in disbelief.

"Forbid? Daddy, you've been encouraging me to write the book!"

Her brown eyes wide, Amanda commented, "PaPa, you'll like Mom's story. There's a really cute part where you take her to the New Orleans zoo to visit Tima the Elephant."

Her usual doting grandfather paid Amanda no attention.

"Good grief, Daddy!" I said getting up. "I'll show you the proofs this very minute. There is absolutely nothing you wouldn't want me to say."

My father glared and said, "I'm not going to read the book. And I don't want it published."

The three of us sat in stunned silence as my daddy finished his meal. As for Jamey, Amanda, and me, most of our "Welcome to Atlanta dinner" would be thrown in the garbage. Well practiced in the skill of diffusing tension, I pulled myself together and chirped, "How about some dessert?"

My stomach was churning. As if nothing had been said, I added, "Daddy, I know you love ice cream. Chocolate or butter pecan?"

As we got ready for bed, my father snored contentedly in the next room.

"Damn, Baby Doll, that was pretty intense."

"Now I know why Daddy's wife didn't come with him. She must be upset about my book. I'll bet she had some major input into his change of heart."

"Come here," said Jamey. "Let me give you a hug."

After I took my father to the airport, I came home and fell to pieces. The next morning I called Pam.

"I know how dear your daddy is," she lamented. "What's happened to him?"

"Daddy is not always himself lately. I noticed his temper when I was in Memphis, and he lashed out at some poor waitress."

Writer, Writer

Pam's reaction was one of surprise, softened with sympathy. "I'm sorry," she said. "I'm just so sorry."

"Me, too." I wanted to cry, but I didn't. The truth was Mercer was ready to go to press with *Scar*. There was nothing I could do other than make corrections or add a few sentences here and there. What my friend said next freed me from Daddy's angry edict. Pam, always an objective confidante remarked, "As I see it, your father forfeited his control over you when he left you in charge of your mother."

"Thank you," I replied. Then I did cry.

Knowing I wouldn't be sharing the book with my father, I went back and reread pages which included Harvey Clark. He remained the charming and ambitious salesman, initially a loving husband, and always a proud parent. I reworked other sections adding honest revelations regarding Harvey's neglect of his family.

When I talked with the marketing people at Mercer Press, I made one request.

"Please don't release any publicity in Memphis."

I hung up the phone and leaned back in my chair. All I could do was shake my head and wonder. Would the drama ever end?

Writer, Writer

Red Eyes

Scar came out in spring 2001. People who kindly hosted parties for *Charlotte Street* graciously offered similar festivities for the new book. I declined explaining this was more like a second wedding. Jamey and I decided on a small event in our backyard. It would give the Man of My Dreams an opportunity to show off his new garden.

Our intimate gathering grew in biblical proportions. With excellent culinary assistance from the generous members of my bridge club, we entertained more than two hundred guests on a Sunday afternoon. Praise be! The weather was perfect.

Readers responded differently to *Scar*. With *Charlotte Street*, I was always tickled pink when people said they liked my work. With *Scar*, readers not only made pleasing comments; but they also hugged me.

Some said, "Poor thing."

More often, it was, "I've been down your road. Let's have a cup of coffee."

One person invited me to a business lunch. I arrived early, grabbed a prime seat on the patio, ordered iced tea, and looked over the menu. After a few minutes, I checked the time. My lunch date hadn't appeared. I'm the person who tends to run late. Was I at the wrong restaurant?

Wrong day, incorrect time? Had something happened to him? Traffic? A wreck?

"Sorry," shouted the man as he hurried across the patio. Greeting me with a kiss on my cheek, he seated himself making reference to his red eyes.

Rubbing my own itchy eyes, I blamed the pollen.

My friend studied me. His demeanor was more serious than I'd come to expect from him. He cleared his throat.

"Milam, my eyes aren't red from allergies. I've been crying."

"Oh no! What's wrong?"

"It's actually what's right," he said. "I've spent the last two days reading your book."

I put my hand to my chest.

"Like your family, mine has a good bit of healing to do. Because of your story, I called my brother this morning." He paused. "It's the first time we've talked in years."

Tears welled up in my eyes.

"We had a good conversation. It's a beginning."

I nodded with a smile. "I'm happy for you and for your brother."

We ordered lunch, and, as planned, discussed business.

Writer, Writer

If no other person on the planet understands my message, this friend's breakthrough with his brother made my difficult struggle worth it.

Milam McGraw Propst

Writer, Writer

Almost Caught

Eight weeks after *Scar* came out, I was honored with a party in Valdosta, Georgia. Our friend Margaret had read the first version, *Are You in There, Momma,* and liked it. So when I told her about *Scar*, she invited me to speak at her annual Book Review.

Jamey was equally enthusiastic about our trip, because he would get to play golf with Margaret's husband, Phil. While I chatted with the fifteen or so women I'd anticipated coming, he'd be on the golf course making birdies.

I was astonished when Margaret and I walked in their country club and saw not a dozen ladies but an audience of sixty. She is known for hosting spectacular gatherings, and this was no exception. I felt like a real super star.

After I spoke, we enjoyed a divine Southern luncheon complete with chicken salad and cheese straws. Fresh cut flowers decorated eight lace-clothed tables. We were served a scrumptiously sinful chocolate dessert chock full of calories.

Eating is another benefit of my career. "I work for food" could become my slogan.

After lunch, I'd planned to sign books and talk one on one with some of the audience. I hoped my story might inspire other women whose own wounds could benefit from encouragement and healing.

As plates were cleared, a lady raised her hand and stood to speak.

"I can't wait to buy your book. I grew up in Memphis, so some of the locations you mentioned are familiar to me."

"It's always fun to meet people from home," I responded asking her maiden name, where she'd grown up, and which school she'd attended. Oblivious to the other fifty-eight ladies sipping decaf coffee, our conversation turned into old home week.

"In fact, I'm going to buy two copies."

Taking her seat, she added, "One's for me, and the other is for another Memphian."

The possibility of my knowing the person would be a coincidence of mammoth proportions. Nonetheless I asked her friend's name.

"Paula McEniry."

My eyes shot from their sockets. I screamed, "Paula McEniry!"

Every conversation screeched to a halt. Ice could be heard melting in glasses as women froze in their seats.

"Surely you can't mean Bobby's wife?"

"Why yes! Only he's called Bob these days."

Writer, Writer

"I'm sorry, so sorry; but you can NOT give Paula my book!"

"Why not?"

"Trust me; you must promise. I could be killed!"

"Killed?"

Everyone leaned forward in their seats.

"Sorry, I'm exaggerating," I stuttered, forcing a laugh. "After all, I am a writer."

My face was on fire. My voice went up several octaves.

"You see, Bobby's, errr, Bob's dad is my father's best friend. The two were in business together and go to lunch every week. I know this sounds weird, but Daddy cannot know my book's been published."

I looked at the sea of stricken faces. Their mouths hanging open, the ladies had to wonder what happened to their formerly articulate speaker. Like Dr. Jekyll, I'd transformed into a drooling Mrs. Hyde.

Mercifully this was a group of Southern women. We are a unique breed of female. Gothic is a lifestyle for many raised in the South. Our secrets nourish us like mother's milk. We are also exceptionally polite.

Cheerful chatter gradually resumed. More decaf was served. Several ladies asked for second helpings of dessert. I was one of them.

We sold a ton of books.

A couple weeks later, I flew to Memphis to visit Daddy and his wife. We were sitting in their den talking about absolutely nothing, our most comfortable topic. As we discussed the day's forecast for rain and planned what we'd watch on television after the noon news, I noticed a stack of magazines on the table between the two, Daddy and his wife. On top of the pile was Mercer Press's spring catalogue. My heart skipped several beats. Our copy had already arrived, so I knew it contained a promotion for *It May Not Leave a Scar*.

"Milam!"

"Daddy!" I jerked nearly falling out of my chair.

"It's almost time for *Golden Girls*."

"Great, I love that show," I tweeted back cheerfully as if I weren't having a full blown stroke. I prayed for a solution while Betty White, Rue McClanahan, and Bea Arthur fought a funny case of flu. Can flu be funny? They made it so. Laughing helped me breathe.

Daddy started to snore, and his wife excused herself to their bedroom for a nap. I seized the opportunity. I crept like a cat burglar toward his recliner and slipped the catalogue between the covers of *USA Today*.

"Humfff," snorted my father.

I clutched the booty to my chest.

"Where are you going?" he asked.

Writer, Writer

"To the bathroom. Be right back."

I wrapped the catalogue in my dirty clothes and placed it in the bottom of my suitcase. The mother of three almost adult children, I was behaving like a devious teenager.

"Oh, hell," said Daddy. "I dozed off and missed the end of *Golden Girls*."

"You didn't miss a thing, Daddy." I leaned over and kissed him on his forehead.

I never ceased worrying our phone would ring one day. I'd hear my father's voice on the other end. Mad as the devil, Daddy would say, "Who the hell is Harvey Clark?"

Writer, Writer

Momma's Political Opinions

Writing about family dysfunction doesn't always have to remain so dismal. Oddly often for me, humor punctuates the process. I might have continued to fret over my father and his wife, or I could switch gears and craft a piece to make myself chuckle. The following story about my mother's take on politics proves the point.

At first glance, Momma's opinions sound narrow-minded, ignorant, and ridiculous. Looking back, her attitudes are well, pretty funny. Never a person interested in politics, she only voted one time in her entire life. She voted for Dwight David Eisenhower for thirty-fourth president of the United States. Because my mother was sincerely grateful the five-star general succeeded in bringing her husband home from Germany, she decided the man might do a reasonably good job running the country.

For years she kept an "I Like Ike" button in her jewelry box. I recall pinning the button on my Terry Lee doll. This was extremely inappropriate because the doll was made in Germany. For sure, Terry Lee would not have liked Ike.

Momma, contrary to the views of many women in the United States, thought Mamie Eisenhower's bangs were darling. A bit tipsy one afternoon, she decided to cut some for me as a tribute to the First Lady.

"You'll look adorable," said my mother as she pulled the comb across the top of my head parting my hair. Momma came at my face with my grandmother's sewing scissors.

I could smell beer on her breath. I held my own.

"Sit still, Milam!"

"Yes, Momma."

I looked in the bathroom mirror. The front of my hair was getting shorter and shorter and more and more crooked. Even so, I didn't chance moving my lips to complain lest I distract her. The snipping scissors were dangerously close to my eyes.

"Don't move. I'm trying to trim the other side."

I stiffened my shoulders to hold steady my neck.

"Milam, I never noticed before; but one of your eyes seems lower than the other."

"Momma, do I look ugly?"

"No, Milam, I'm only kidding. You look exactly like your father."

I couldn't decide if looking like Daddy was a good thing or not. What was crystal clear, my bangs were a disaster.

"Hell, I can't do this."

Momma spit in her hand and ran it across my forehead to smooth my chopped hair to the side. She grabbed a bobby pin and secured my bangs, or absence thereof, into place.

"Want some ice cream?"

"Yes, please."

My bangs eventually grew out.

Momma had neither the time nor the patience for politics after the years following WWII. Even if she had been a registered voter in 1976, she would not have joined Jimmy Carter's Peanut Brigade.

First of all, the naval officer, peanut farmer turned senator, then governor of Georgia had not played a part in the D-Day invasion, let alone plan it as had General Eisenhower.

My mother disapproved of our president so unyieldingly; she refused to eat peanut butter the whole time Mr. Carter was in the White House. Part of the problem was Momma didn't like his name.

"Jimmy is a childish name for a man with political ambitions," she complained. "He should go by James."

Momma may have formed her opinion about nicknames based on her own mother's prejudices. B had made a similar statement when I introduced her to my future husband. After Jamey left our house, B took me aside and said, "Your young man is perfectly charming and very handsome, but I think he should be called by his given name. James would be far more appropriate were he to run for president."

I didn't pass along my grandmother's suggestion. I was fairly certain politics was not in Jamey's future.

As for Jimmy Carter, the gentleman never had an opportunity to hear either woman's advice. Perhaps if he had, Mr. Carter might have been elected to a second term.

The real problem between Jimmy Carter and my mother wasn't with the President of the United States himself, but with his younger brother, Billy.

Not only was the president's brother well known for marketing his own brand, *Billy Beer,* but he was also famous or infamous for his consumption of the beverage. In 1979, Billy Carter courageously admitted himself into an alcohol rehabilitation facility. What is noteworthy is the man wisely took steps to deal with his problem.

"It's disgusting," condemned my mother.

"To think the president's brother would make such a public spectacle of himself. The Carter family must be absolutely humiliated. I feel sorry for the whole damn bunch."

Billy Carter would overcome his alcoholism.

So did Momma.

Writer, Writer

Swapping Pedestals

Momma and I were slowly rebuilding an adult friendship, Jamey and I were doing well, our children were busy with their own lives, and my creative ventures were truly fulfilling. But in the sacred sanctuary of our home, the beasts from my childhood would creep in to take an occasional bite out of me. All of a sudden, I would smell stale cigarette smoke in the exhale of an alcoholic's breath.

I needed a break. "Nestle."

Returning after a quick walk with the dog, I rallied.

"How could you?" I repeated settling back into my chair.

Once again, how could *who*? Momma? No, not my mother.

"How could Daddy? Yes, Daddy!"

It hit me like a sledgehammer. I was angry with my father. As Momma's pedestal began to rise, the pedestal on which I'd always kept Daddy plummeted.

My father had always traveled for business, for his all important job. He'd started off as an office boy and worked his way up. For fifty years, he'd worked for Linde Company, a division of Union Carbide.

"Linde. Linde." I spit the company's name as I would a sarcastic mantra.

Writer, Writer

Daddy had to travel, didn't he? Yes, of course, he did. He said so every time he packed his suitcase. Momma and I got to be with him on weekends, Friday night until Monday morning. Two days should have been enough for my mother and me.

No, two days was not enough! I sat fuming.

"How are things going?"

The sound of Jamey's voice made me jump.

"Fine," I snapped.

"It's getting late. Are you at a stopping point?"

"Guess so. Who won the Falcon's game?" I could not have cared less. We went to bed, and I had horrible nightmares. Wolves in mirrors? I couldn't recall. When the morning sun finally broke through the blinds, our sheets were a tangled mess.

Jamey asked what was wrong. I must have kept him awake.

"Nothing."

I brushed my teeth with way too much vigor. I spit blood in the sink and went to the kitchen to start breakfast. Jamey left for the bank, and I returned to my desk. I sipped hot tea and thought how grateful I was my husband never had much business travel. The few times he was gone, I'd struggled. I counted the days until he returned home safely.

Safely for him? No, safely for me.

In 1966, my single caveat to Jamey's marriage proposal had not been about having children, or religion, or whether or not we would move to Timbuktu.

I squealed a most definite "Yes, yes, yes," and cautiously added, "But please, Jamey Propst, please promise you will never, ever travel."

Ironically, Jamey did leave for one horribly long year. I still have nightmares he is ordered to return to Vietnam. I admit, "It does leave a scar." I must acknowledge real life, with its trials and triumphs, provides material for us writers.

My husband has a gift for getting right to the point in difficult situations. An example occurred shortly after I'd begrudgingly assumed responsibility for Momma. Jamey and I had gone for a quiet ride to calm me down after a particularly stressful day. He listened as I ranted on and on about my parent's divorce, Daddy's new marriage, and my constant anxiety surrounding my mother's care. I'd talked for thirty minutes without a pause.

He stopped the car and said, "Baby Doll, your daddy stuck you with Mary Catherine when you were four-years-old."

The truth cut through me like a meat cleaver. My new challenge was going to be forgiving my father. I spoke not a word the whole way home. I wandered into my study

Writer, Writer

and picked up my Mary Engelbreit doll. Wearing a mean scowl on her face, the doll clutches a message in her right hand, "Snap out of it."

"You're right, Mary Engelbreit. I must."

Blue Bird

The day was a pleasant one until I got the call . . . darn telephone. When I was attempting to look after my aging parents and juggle adult children, the phone's screaming ring shot through me like bullets. Prior to the days of caller ID, somehow I knew this one meant trouble. I grabbed the telephone.

Daddy's wife was on the other end. Mary Engelbreit's words, "Snap out of it" popped like soap bubbles.

I was needed in Memphis right away. My father was hospitalized. Again.

Not intending to sound mean spirited, but after retiring from Linde, Bill McGraw was bored; so he embarked on a second career visiting doctors and caregivers. After a morning's appointment, he and his wife would eat lunch out, usually enjoying a cheeseburger, fries, and a martini. Every now and then, my father hit the jackpot and was sent for couple days stay in the hospital.

I bought my ticket to Memphis and packed a suitcase. To get my head screwed on straight, I took Nestle for a walk. As we made our way up Franklin Road, I ranted and raved at God.

"I'm too busy with work."

"Jamey and I have tickets for a play."

Writer, Writer

"We were supposed to meet the children for dinner."

I made a laundry list of reasons my father's hospitalization was cramping my style. Nestle stopped to sniff a bush.

"This is another false alarm."

At that moment, a bluebird flew so close to my face, I could feel the flutter of his wings.

"What the heck!" Ducking, I tripped over the dog.

Bluebirds are significant to many people. My friend Jody is one. Some see the brightly colored birds as angels, as emissaries from the Lord. I know, because I'm one of them too.

"Okay, God, I'm listening."

Taking a deep breath I realized I was being anxious, selfish, judgmental, and certainly not a devoted daughter. I always had my father fooled. He thought of me as a sweetheart. I vowed to work on my bad attitude.

Once on board Delta, however, I lost my resolve. I imagined Mary Engelbreit's face frowning at me. Was that a bluebird perched on her shoulder? Even so, I did not want to go to Daddy's bedside and all but prayed for the plane to crash.

We were circling Memphis when a voice came over the loudspeaker.

"Ladies and gentlemen, this is your pilot speaking. There's a thunderstorm over the airport, and we are unable to land. We'll be flying to Huntsville to refuel. I am sorry for any inconvenience this may cause."

My first thought was my daddy was going to be furious.

Always prompt, he was never one to be patient with latecomers. This was before cell phones, so I couldn't let him know what was happening. I envisioned my father sitting in a hospital bed, thumping his fingers on the tray positioned over his lap. With every passing minute, he'd be barking, "Where in the hell is Milam?"

My second thought was about the thunderstorm. I'd prayed not to land; and as a result, every person onboard might die. My co-dependency in full tilt, I accepted total responsibility for a fiery crash somewhere between Memphis and Huntsville. Had the turbulence not kept us buckled in our seats, I may have stood up to address my fellow passengers.

"Everyone, I'm sorry. I prayed to crash. Blame your impending deaths on me."

Thankfully, I remained seated and quiet. I did whisper a prayer. "Lord, You know me, I'm an overly dramatic writer. Please let us survive."

If memory serves, we landed in Huntsville and took on fuel. What I clearly recall is we were several hours late arriving in Memphis. All I could think about was getting a rental car and facing Daddy's music.

"Sorry, ma'am. All the cars are rented."

How could this happen? I was cursed. Or was I cursing? Both.

The woman looked warily at me. "I do have one older model, ma'am. It's an ugly color."

"I'll take it!"

I gave her my credit card, signed the paperwork, grabbed the keys, and made a beeline to parking space number fifty-six. With a streetlight shining on the rattletrap's wet hood, I noticed its color. My rental car was the bluest blue I've ever seen. Bluebird blue.

Arriving at the hospital, I scurried to my father's room. As I often did back in those days, I'd worried needlessly. Omitting any incriminating parts, I recounted the harrowing tale about our near fatal crash. My daddy smiled gently.

"Thank you for coming, Honey. You're my best girl."

I leaned over and hugged him. "I'm glad to be here, Daddy."

He stayed in the hospital for several days. As anticipated, his tests indicated nothing was wrong. I sincerely wish I could visit my father again, even in a hospital. I'd gladly risk another rough plane ride.

I tend to lose rental cars in enormous hospital parking lots. That time, however, whenever I left to pick up our lunch or dinner, the bluebird car was easy for me to find.

It was evident God's little blue angels had been surrounding me all along.

Writer, Writer

White Lies

Back from Memphis, I had time to think, which was not always healthy for me. I'd written a book about secrets and how keeping those secrets all but destroyed the lives of my grandmother and my mother. Yet there I was keeping one of my own, the publishing of *Scar*, from Daddy.

I had been well schooled in the craft of deception. Wasn't I into my forties before I learned about my grandfather's suicide? The death of Charles Lawrence Whitman was not from an automobile wreck as I was told. So badly injured was he, his only solution was a self-inflicted bullet wound. I wish someone had shared the truth sooner. Secrets have a way of eating at people.

I liked to believe a white lie is all together different. It's a tiny omission, not an atrocious miscarriage of the truth. A white lie is a convenient way to skirt reality. Daddy didn't know about *Scar*, just as I'd kept his second marriage from Momma. My father and his wife insisted I not tell her they were married, and I complied. I dreaded my mother's response, rage or a drinking binge, or far worse, her broken spirit. With the suggestion from a psychiatrist and the agreement of a Catholic priest, I practiced my answer in front of our bedroom mirror.

Writer, Writer

When she asked, "Where is the old fool?"

"What old fool might you mean?"

"Your father, of course!"

I replied with well rehearsed words, "Gee, Momma, I don't really know. The last time I heard from him, I believe he was calling from Florida."

Momma never brought up the subject again. So ingrained are those words in my mind, I may repeat them on my death bed.

The score: two white lies and counting.

Had Daddy read *Scar*, he might have been pleased. I know he would have appreciated how my putting the story on paper had helped me heal. On the other hand, my father and his wife might have misconstrued every word and viewed the book as an attack on them. Elderly and wounded in their own lives, they may not have been capable of understanding the story's message.

Thankfully, my book would remain a white lie.

A greeting card on the bookcase caught my eye. It wasn't one I intended for a friend. Its message applied to me. On the front is a confident young girl. She holds a walking stick and has her hand planted firmly on her right hip. Red flowers surround her. Attributed to *anonymous*, it reads, "What does it matter what went before or after? Now with myself, I will begin and end."

To this day, my purpose is to move on from the past while not obsessing about the future. I try to do so with honesty and with a sense of humor.

No more white lies, only wit.

Writer, Writer

Dearly Departed

I still feel an occasion twinge of guilt about *Scar*.
 Momma used to shake her head at me and say, "I swear, Milam McGraw, you tell everything you know and more besides."

She's right. In *Writer Writer*, I did it again.

My parents, the three of them, Momma, Daddy, and B have been dead for many years. My grandmother's death in 1985 was followed my mother's in 1998. To fulfill her wish, we buried Momma near her beloved father. She had yearned to be with him for sixty-six years.

Daddy passed away from a sudden heart attack in 2001, only sixteen days before his first great grandchild would be born. How eagerly Bill McGraw had anticipated becoming a great-grandfather.

I miss my family, Momma, Daddy, and B. They made up the perfect team to raise me. Not only did each of my parents pass on her or his unique talents and characteristics, but each of them contributed to my becoming an author.

Writer, Writer

Part II

Writer, Writer

Stars in My Eyes

Charlotte Street and *Scar* were sold, signed, and residing
on people's bookshelves. I finally considered myself to be
an authentic writer. I no longer had to search for comedy in
bad situations, because my life looked bright, even without
my rose colored glasses.

I was at work on the sequel to *Charlotte Street*.
Ociee's readers had questioned what might happen next;
and, in Sister Thomas Margaret's letter praising the book,
she insisted Ociee return to Mississippi. If that wasn't
pressure enough, author Terry Kay agreed with my English
teacher.

For me professionally, things couldn't get better. So
I thought.

Jamey and Jay were walking out the door en route
to a Braves baseball game. I jokingly said, "Why don't you
guys skip the game and come to Beverly's art show with
me?"

"Are they serving beer?" Jamey chuckled as he
turned to our son. "Jay, it's too hot for baseball anyway."

"Fine with me, Dad. I'd like to see Mrs. Key's
work."

Writer, Writer

The Bennett Street gallery was packed with Beverly's family, friends, and enthusiastic art lovers. Voices were humming in praise as we entered. I made a beeline toward my friend.

"Look at this crowd! I'm so proud of you."

Ever humble, she smiled sweetly. "Thanks."

Jay was on the far side of the gallery having a conversation with one of the Key's sons. I was admiring one particularly appealing painting, a soothing watercolor, when I heard Jamey's voice.

"Steve Dirkes, is that you?"

"Propst? Jamey Propst? What in the world are you doing at an art exhibit?"

"Beverly is Milam's friend," he said gesturing for me to come over.

Steve had worked with Jamey at First Atlanta Bank but found a better fit for his talents as a location director in film. FILM. Jamey and I have always been huge movie buffs. Every weekend we read the reviews in *The Atlanta Journal Constitution* entertainment pages and buy our tickets.

"Nice to see you," I said extending my hand.

Steve introduced us to the two women with him. The sisters, Kristen McGary and Amy McGary, had recently started *CineVita Productions*. We were talking to not one, not two, but three people in the entertainment field! Until recently Amy and Kristen were working in Los Angeles. Hollywood, that is: H-O-L-L-Y-W-O-O-D!

Among the honest-to-gawd movie stars they knew was Tommy Lee Jones. "Tommy Lee is one of my all time favorites!"

I shudder to recall how I ridiculous I must have sounded questioning, giggling, and gushing about moviedom.

On our way home, Jamey suggested I send Steve a copy of *Charlotte Street*.

"His little girls are the perfect ages for your book."

I was first in line at the post office the next day and overnighted my book to Steve's office in nearby Decatur. It must have arrived within hours! Kristen McGary happened by as he opened the package.

"Do you remember Milam, that zany woman at Beverly Key's art show?"

"How could I forget her?"

"This is her book," he said handing *Charlotte Street* to Kristen. Her response prompted Steve to call me.

"After my girls are finished with your novel, I'd like to pass it along to Kristen McGary."

"Steve, keep yours, but please give me Kristen's address. I'd like to mail her a copy."

I went at once to overnight two additional books, one for Kristen and a second for Amy. The expense was worth every penny. A week later, I was having lunch with the McGary sisters at Anis Café & Bistro.

I continued to pump the women about Hollywood. "Which of you lived next door to Brad Pitt?"

"Amy, Steve mentioned you'd won an Emmy for *The Oldest Living Confederate Widow*. Is it true?"

"Yes, in fact, I did."

Kristen shared a great tidbit about when her sister's name was called at the award ceremony. Instead of handing Amy her acceptance speech, Kristen mistakenly gave her their parking ticket! I lapped up every word of her "inside story."

"About Tommy Lee . . ."

Kristen silenced me. "What we want to discuss, Milam, is your book."

"My book? O-o-o-cieeee?"

We were dining outside on the patio. I vaguely remember the waiter helping me down from a tree.

"Yes, Ociee," she began. "Amy and I have always wanted to work together on a film, especially on a family film. We believe your grandmother's story would be perfect for us."

"You want to make a movie from my book?"

"We do."

I had landed in the middle of a madwoman's wildest dream. I remember nothing about the day, our meal, or anyone else dining at Anis. What I do recall is shrieking, "Yes!"

Gathering my composure, I asked, "How much do you charge?"

The women laughed. "Dear, we pay you for the movie rights."

"Really?"

"Really."

I called Marc Jolley.

Flabbergasted, he said, "We've never had a movie from a Mercer book!"

I grinned so wide my lips cracked. "Now you will."

With stars twinkling in my eyes, I drove to Athens for lunch with Terry Kay. The author of countless novels, one of his most famous, *To Dance with the White Dog,* had been made into a marvelous movie starring Jessica Tandy and Hume Cronyn. I couldn't wait to tell him my news.

Terry Kay can be something of a skeptic and is fiercely protective of other writers. He's particularly concerned about me. He considers me a nitwit when it comes to business. He's right.

"Milam, tell me," began Terry. "Who are these women?"

Writer, Writer

I shared everything about Beverly's show, Steve, and the meeting with the McGary sisters.

"Okay."

"Kristen owns an apartment in LA. She and Amy hobnob with all sorts of famous people."

"I see."

Terry's phone rang. He politely excused himself to the kitchen. I kept my seat but checked out the interesting memorabilia throughout the room. Momma didn't term me "Nosy Rosie" without good reason. On the coffee table was a black wooden frame holding four photographs of an elderly gentleman. In one shot, the man is posed with a large white dog.

I gasped.

My host returned. "Sorry about the interruption. That was my daughter."

"Not to worry, Terry. My children come first, too."

He nodded.

I could contain myself no longer. I pointed to the picture. "Terry, is this your father with THE white dog?"

"Yes, my wife framed it for me. Nice job. She has a shop in Stone Mountain."

Then, almost as an aside, he added, "It's the only picture we have of Daddy with the dog."

The Holy Grail! It was a good thing I was all gushed out, or I would have made a fool of myself. Again, I appreciated the man's initial thought was to give credit to his wife for her work. The curmudgeon Terry pretends to be, he is a devoted family man.

"Back to our problem," he said.

"Problem?"

"To begin with, what are these women paying you for the rights to your book?"

"Terry, I didn't even understand that's how things work. I offered to pay them."

Terry grumbled, "Milam, exactly what does your contract say about film rights?"

"No clue."

He positioned his hands on the top of his head as if to keep his brain from shooting up to the ceiling.

"Call your publisher," said Terry with a sigh. "Demand at least fifty percent. Now let's go get a sandwich."

I returned to Atlanta.

"Marc, I met with Terry Kay today."

"He's a very nice man," replied my publisher.

"Yes, he is. Here's the deal," I cleared my throat. "I'm going to ask Mercer for fifty percent for the book rights to the movie."

Silence.

Writer, Writer

Then came a belly rumbling laugh. "Milam, that's fine with me. Your contract calls for you to receive eighty-five percent!"

"Oh."

In my thank you note to Terry, I mentioned negotiating Mercer up to eighty-five percent. I'm certain Mr. Kay had quite a laugh at my expense.

Full Circle

Writing takes time. Lots of time. The process can be even slower for beginners. It took me twenty years to put my first serious sentences on paper.

And there's editing which, in my opinion, is the core of the craft. After months of typing, I pitched the first three chapters of Ociee's story and started anew with the gypsy scene. My second novel, *Scar,* is but a shadow of the original draft. Initially, I rewrote the novel spinning fact into fiction. In a second revision, I deleted every word not vital to my message. For me, thorough editing is the most crucial stage in the writing process.

After writing and editing seven books, I honestly believed I understood my job. I did not! *Writer, Writer* started coming together only after both Marc and my editor, Letitia Sweitzer, suggested I focus on a central theme. I listened to them and deleted more than one hundred pages.

Timing is also a key factor. A writer needs to be motivated and ready to write or nothing happens. My long hikes with Nestle, and now with our lab mix Bella, are not solely for exercise. A brisk walk clears cobwebs from my brain. I can return from our outings with fresh ideas and eager to work.

Destiny certainly played a critical role in my career. The tiny roots for the Ociee film sprouted far back in early

Writer, Writer

1980, when Jamey and I saw *Cotton Patch Gospel* for the first time.

"Jamey, I'm ordering tickets," I said waving the newspaper in his face. "Look here, Harry Chapin wrote the songs for a musical at the Alliance. We're going on Saturday!"

The creator and star of the then one-man show, Tom Key, was astounding as he played some twenty plus characters. At the show's conclusion, the audience sprang to its feet, roaring with applause. So did the Propsts. For the next fifteen years, we saw everything in which Tom appeared from *Cotton Patch* and *Blood Knot* to *To Kill a Mockingbird* and *Red*.

We've also had opportunities to hear Tom speak. During one speech, he talked about Harry Chapin. Tom revealed the brilliant songwriter had completed his work on *Cotton Patch* only days before his fatal accident. The "what if" shook me to my soul. Tom Key's performance which ignited my creative course might never have been.

In the early nineties, as Amanda, William, and Jay were taking flight from our family nest, I was blooming in my classes at Oglethorpe. Sixty pages into the Ociee story, Dorothy Brooks invited me to her women's group. The ladies were stretching their artistic muscles with the help of a creative workbook, *The Artist Way*.

I jumped at the opportunity.

Dorothy welcomed me and opened the meeting with one of her latest poems. The other members introduced themselves. Our hostess, Lalor, talked about her dreams to write and reach out to women as a spiritual mentor. Janet described herself as being all over the place. An actress, a comedian and writer, she did voice-over commercials, played drums, sang, and played in a rock 'n roll band with her husband Tommy, famous for writing the theme song for *WKRP in Cincinnati*.

Sitting quietly to my right was an unassuming young woman named Beverly. A painter, she mentioned growing up in Fairhope, Alabama, and graduating from the University of Alabama.

Lalor asked me to introduce myself.

"Thank you, girls, for having me. Roll Tide, Beverly. I'm a Bama girl, too."

She nodded.

"I'm an empty-nester writing a novel," I began cautiously.

"On Saturdays, my husband Jamey goes to the golf course. I stay home happily playing with words. As you might assume, I'm right-brained, while Jamey is left-brained. I confuse him, the poor man."

Beverly spoke up. "I don't know which is worse. My husband and I are both right-brained. We get lost everywhere we go." She giggled, "But we have a wonderful time getting there!"

Everyone laughed.

"What does your husband do?"

The women frowned at me in disbelief.

"Beverly KEY," said Janet. "Her husband is Tom Key."

"Tom Key!" I rose to my full height, flapping my arms like a colossal crane.

"You know Tom Key? Well, I guess you do," I stammered. "You're married to him."

The women looked at me like I had recently flown in from Planet Zurk. I wanted the floor to swallow me.

"Ladies, shall we begin our meeting?" offered Lalor.

We opened our workbooks.

Creative women are an accepting breed. Even after my social meltdown, the ladies asked me to join their group. That uncomfortable encounter began my friendship with Beverly.

The five of us blossomed in *The Artist Way*. Lalor discovered her perfect path, while Janet became even more successful. Dorothy has had poetry published along with having her short story included in a best selling anthology.

As for Beverly, she is now a well established painter. Her work hangs in homes and businesses around the country. Jamey and I are fortunate to own several pieces. I'm looking at one of her watercolors to the left of my desk. The soft greens and grays of a mountain stream provide me with pleasant visual breaks from my computer screen. Never will I forget it was at Beverly's art show we met the McGary sisters.

Without Dorothy, I would not have joined *The Artist Way* and have gotten to know Lalor, Janet, and Beverly.

Without Beverly, we would not have run into Steve Dirkes.

Without Steve, we would not have met Kristen McGary and Amy McGary.

Without Harry Chapin's connection to *Cotton Patch*, we may not have discovered Tom Key.

Had I not been captivated by Harry's singing the Chapin family anthem, *All My Life's a Circle*, none of these fortuitous things would have come to pass.

God had His perfect plan mapped out for me. All my life's a circle.

Writer, Writer

The Movie Set

I was on my way to the Mitchell farm for the first day of shooting *The Adventures of Ociee Nash*. I pinched myself.

"B, the dream is coming true just like I promised!"

Even having zero sense of direction, I didn't get lost. I followed the posters marked "Ociee." The film's associate producer, our friend Steve, had strategically placed signs to guide the cast, the crew, and this befuddled writer through every twist and turn on the back roads of the picturesque farmland south of Atlanta.

I felt B's presence. As when I was a little girl, my grandmother was leading me to her home in Marshall County, Mississippi.

The signs ended at a roped-off pasture. I parked my car; and excitedly shaking from head to toe, I started down a tree framed dirt driveway. I walked past tractor trailer trucks and things indicative of making a movie. In the distance, I spotted the Mitchell's weathered barn and started the journey back to the late 1800's.

I paused. How like my mother-in-law's barn was the Mitchell's! Even though Nicholsville, Alabama, Mary Loftin Propst's childhood home was six hours away, it felt as if I'd set foot on Loftin land. Mary's farm is sacred ground on which our family has built many cherished memories. Her homeplace provided my inspiration for the Nash farm. The kitchen was Grandmother Cora Loftin's kitchen. The porch was where we sat to string the beans and listen to tall tales from Jamey's cousin, Sam. Ociee's bedroom was the front room off the porch, the one in which Jamey, our children, and I slept every Thanksgiving. It's the same room where Jamey's father, Ed, came in to stoke the wood fire on freezing November mornings.

Walking toward the house with its welcoming front porch, the out buildings, the rolling pastures, vegetable gardens, and fruit trees, I was not only transported to Nicholsville but also to Marshall County, Mississippi.

The year was 1898. The farm was busier than a beehive.

"Howdy, ma'am," said the darling Bill Butler. He reached out his hand to mine. "I'm Ben Nash."

"Well, Ben, how do you do?"

"Mighty fine. Thank you, ma'am."

Kristen waved cheerfully at me and motioned for the young actor to get into position. I stood and watched as the Nash children gathered. Was my grandmother overlooking the farm scene? Did she notice when her brother, Ben, said hello to me? Had she seen their older brother, Fred? Did she recognize herself?

I thought back to the evening Charlotte Street won "Georgia Author of the Year for a First Novel." I stood clutching the microphone and thanked everyone from the Lord to Marc Jolley. Of course, I saluted my grandmother.

"Look, B, surely you can see us from your cloud in Heaven!" I'd said. "Thank you for your story."

Could the movie somehow be a gift from my grandmother and from Momma and Daddy as well? Was this a heavenly hello from the three of them?

A light drizzle cut through the mist. I spotted Marc Jolley. He stood under an umbrella watching Kristen speak with the actors. It was my custom to greet him with a hug, but this time he waved me away.

"Don't," he warned, "you'll make me cry."

Bless the tender man. I owed him everything. Marc was the first professional person to have faith in my grandmother's story. When Mercer published *Charlotte Street*, we also shared an outlandish dream of what a marvelous movie it would make. There was almost too much emotion to absorb.

Marc cleared his throat, "You and I always hoped this would happen."

"And here we are," I replied

Moisture rolled down Marc's cheek. Rain? More likely it was a tear.

Writer, Writer

The star of *The Adventures of Ociee Nash* was new discovery, Skyler Day. Following the screen tests of some two hundred young actresses from Los Angeles to Savannah, the Cumming, Georgia native was deemed perfect for the part. Skyler could act; and she was smart, well prepared, adorable, and endearing.

My grandmother would approve.

The first day of shooting, Skyler produced a "cuss box."

"Anyone who says a bad word has to contribute a dollar."

At the wrap party, the traditional celebration at the end of filming, the young actress arrived with a beautifully wrapped package in hand. Presenting the gift to Kristen, Skyler said, "I used cuss box money to buy a present for our director."

Kristen turned beet red, "I hope I didn't contribute all the money!"

There is a less public demonstration of how beautifully the Days were raising their daughter. I had an opportunity to chat with Skyler's mother, Kelly, and posed a question.

"It's really none of my business, but what would you do if stardom goes to Skyler's head?"

Without batting an eye, the cool, calm, and collected mother arched her back, "That's easy. We'll go back to Cumming."

The Days have since moved to Los Angeles where Skyler and her twin brother, Dalton, are acting, singing, composing, and playing guitar. As I write this book, Skyler has a recurring role on the television series, *Parenthood*.

Jamey and I had the pleasant experience of hearing the twins perform during the recent holidays. After their concert, Skyler told me a secret.

"Our movie really spoiled me for all future work, Miss Milam. Everyone involved in *Ociee* was so very nice to us!"

Dalton has a small part in the film. He plays one of the young Asheville boys, who can't quite figure out how to handle the feisty Mississippi tomboy. He's in the creek scene with other young actors including Lucas Till in the role of a boyish Harry Vanderbilt.

Anytime I speak to school children about the making of the movie, they get a kick out of learning the McGarys hired animal actors. Students are particularly surprised to discover there are not only professional horses and dogs, but also professional pigs, cows, and chickens.

However, it was an amateur, a golden retriever, who landed the biggest non-human part. Woofer belonged to production coordinator, Stephanie Ryan. She brought her friendly pooch to work with her every day, and he won over the crew.

Kristen asked me if the Nash family's "Gray Dog" could be given a different name.

"Skyler has bonded beautifully with Woofer." She added, "Besides, as an actor, he's a natural."

"Unless you plan to dye his coat, Gray Dog doesn't fit so Woofer it is!"

Woofer would make his film debut and steal a scene or two. The pup became one of the most recognizable stars in the movie. He walked on the Red Carpet, attended the World Premiere, and joined the actors on stage for a well deserved curtain call. Woofer also made numerous public appearances.

The handsome golden has since passed away. The sweet, crowd pleasing pup was one terrific performer.

Bomb Scare

Every day on the farm brought rich memories for me, especially when friends drove down to watch.

For years, Pam Weeks, along with Jackie Brown and Betty George, had prayed for my manuscript to be published. Their prayers were answered with dividends.

Pam and I were standing in the farmhouse kitchen.

"This is unreal," said Pam, shaking her head. She gave me a hug.

"Are we both dreaming?" I asked.

"I don't think so."

"I remember typing about Ociee's stringing 'those dern beans' more than ten years ago."

"I remember reading it."

I snapped a reluctant Pam's picture to capture the moment.

Marilynn Winston's visit took a different twist. She and I stood beside the porch watching a scene between Ociee and the gypsy, John Leon, who is played by Anthony Rodriguez of the Aurora Theater.

"Anthony was born blind in one eye," I told Marilynn; "But he's never allowed it to hold him back."

"Good for him."

Writer, Writer

"The man was so excited about his audition, he forgot to put in his concealing contact lens. What started out as a faux pas quickly became an asset. The McGarys crafted clever dialogue between the gypsy and Ociee making use of the actor's natural eye."

"Quiet on the set."

"That includes us, Marilynn."

We saw Anthony, in full gypsy attire, sitting astride a magnificent black horse. Kristen directed him to wave farewell to Ociee and gallop away holding high a pound cake baked by the McGarys' mother, Dolores.

Kristen's directions were, "Gallop, wave, and do not drop Mom's cake!"

Bless the actor's courage. Until that morning, Anthony had never been on a horse, much less on a galloping horse. And he was attempting to ride the huge animal hands free.

During the crucial moment, a long, slimy snake slithered down the tree between me and the other city slicker, Marilynn.

We jumped backwards screaming bloody murder.

"Cut!"

Marilynn turned to me. "Quick, get the gypsy. He can handle anything."

"I'm afraid Anthony has enough to do just staying on the horse."

"Ladies, is there a problem?" asked an aggravated Kristen.

I pointed to the snake.

"He's harmless," she frowned disapprovingly. "The snake belongs to the Mitchells. He's their pet."

"Sorry, we'll be quiet from now on."

Behave we did and at a safe distance from the snake.

The same cannot be said for some local teenagers. The nearby community was preparing for the annual *Barnesville Buggy Days*. Some young people decided it would be hilarious to phone the police with a pipe bomb threat.

The film's schedule called for an extremely emotional scene in which a distraught Papa, played by Keith Carradine, would tenderly tell his daughter he was sending her to North Carolina. Ociee and Papa took their places on the front porch. Fred and Ben were positioned on either side of them. A pivotal point in the story, every member of the cast and crew was tense with anticipation.

"Quiet on the set."

Papa began, "Ociee, this is about to tear my heart right out of my chest."

Suddenly a helicopter appeared from the north. Looking like a gargantuan dragon fly, it made an atrociously loud noise, a booming "ba-ba-ba-ba-ba-ba."

Writer, Writer

"Cut!"

"What the heck is going on?"

"I'll find out," said Steve.

"Okay, let's try again."

"Quiet on the set."

No sooner had Papa opened his mouth, than another helicopter came over the horizon.

"For Pete's sakes!"

"Let's go one more time."

"Quiet on the set."

Take 3: "Ociee, this is about to tear my heart" . . . . "ba-ba-ba-ba-ba-ba."

Take 4: "Ociee, this is about to" . . . as if on cue, another helicopter appeared with the then familiar "ba-ba-ba-ba-ba-ba."

Take 5: "Ociee, this is". . .

Take 6. Take 7. Take 8. Take 9.

We later found out newscopters from all around the state were checking out the bomb scare in Barnesville.

Keith Carradine burst into laughter. "Kristen, let's re-title your film 'Ociee Goes to Vietnam' and call it a day!"

Writer, Writer

Precious Memories

Misbehave though I did, Kristen and Amy continued to allow me onto their sets including Agnes Scott College, the Tennessee Valley Railroad near Chattanooga, and locations in Buckhead and Inman Park. I went every day of the twenty-day shoot. These remain the best professional moments of my writing life. Watching my characters speak words, words which were born on a yellow legal pad, provided gratification beyond measure. I was brought to tears on several occasions.

While writing my grandmother's story, I had two images for the children's father, George Nash. The essence of his character was based on my father-in-law, Ed Propst. Strong and athletic our "Softie," aptly named, was totally committed to his family. Mirroring Ed, I wrote Ociee's father as a man having a heart almost too big to contain. A second image was that of Tom Key. As I typed the original manuscript, I envisioned Tom driving a wagon hitched to their horse, Maud.

When it came time to cast the roles, Tom would land another choice part, that of the buggy driver, Mr. Lynch. Through Ociee's finagling, her new friend would become Aunt Mamie's gentleman caller. In the last scene, Mr. Lynch removes his hat, and in full sight of the citizens of Asheville, takes Mamie Nash into his arms and plants a kiss on the maiden lady's lips.

Beverly dropped by the set at Agnes Scott College to watch her husband film his scene. Afterwards, I asked her what she thought.

Mrs. Key replied with a blush, "Isn't Tom so handsome!"

That same afternoon, my friend Cynthia came to take pictures of her husband, Bill, who plays a coronet in the brass band saluting the heroic little girl on "Ociee Nash Day." While waiting for the scene to begin, Cynthia caught a glimpse of Mare Winningham. All decked out in Victorian finery to play Aunt Mamie, the actress was talking on her cell phone. My friend, an avowed newshound, couldn't help herself; she eavesdropped.

"It's as if I've landed in a lovely park a century ago!" said the movie star. "You wouldn't believe the gorgeous costumes. This is amazing."

Mare looked up and saw Cynthia. Mortified, but pleased with her scoop, my friend hurried to tell me what she'd heard. I, in turn, passed on Mare's compliments to costume designer, Susan Mickey.

Jackie Brown, friend and proofreader, landed a prime extra's spot as Mrs. Vanderbilt. What speaks volumes about this lady is her daughter, Suzanne was marrying in an out-of-town wedding, less than one week later. Even so, the mother-of-the-bride sat for hours and hours in the hot September sunshine. She wears a gorgeous wool costume and never once stops grinning.

A retired school teacher, Jackie delights in sharing her movie experience with students. "Children, I want you to know one thing, acting is very hard work!"

Jerry Lee Davis, another dear friend and fellow writer, became a jack of all trades. He seemed to be everywhere, from playing a townsperson in the Chattanooga scene to running countless errands for Kristen and Amy. I recently discovered he was once commandeered to comb the hair of male extras. Most importantly, this charming man served as an encourager to everyone who crossed his path.

Jerry Lee joked, "Hell, if something happens to Skyler, I'll put on a blond wig and play Ociee myself!"

Jerry Lee was often by my side. Early on, he snapped a picture of me with Keith Carradine. It was a golden moment as the honest to goodness star took his time to talk to me. He made my day when he said, "Thank you, Milam, for giving me such a great character to play."

A writer's life can't get any better.

A precious older neighbor of ours, the darling Cornelia Jolley drove across town to Agnes Scott one morning at 4:30. That would be 4:30 a.m., in the pitch black dark. Cornelia was in her late eighties at the time. When I noticed her walking from wardrobe dressed in a long black skirt and sporting a big floppy flower-adorned hat, I all but dropped my teeth.

"Cornelia! I didn't know you were scheduled for today. I would have driven you here."

"It's no big deal; I did perfectly fine. Why, I even stopped to gas up my car," she bragged. "You know, dear heart, I wouldn't have let you down for the world."

Vintage Cornelia.

Jerry Lee was standing nearby. Typically for him, he hurried over to greet the elderly Southern Belle.

"Miss Cornelia, I am Jerry Lee Davis, a friend of Milam's. I would be delighted to escort you to the set."

"Thank you, young man."

As they walked away, Jerry Lee accidentally stepped on the hem of Cornelia's skirt.

"Oh, my Lord," he exclaimed. "Miss Cornelia, I about defrocked you!"

She responded, "My dear, it would not have been much of a thrill."

Writer, Writer

Cornelia's second scene takes place at a tearoom in Inman Park. I wanted to do something to thank her for being such a good sport.

"You'd honor us both, Cornelia, if you would wear my grandmother's cameo."

Tears filled her eyes. "It is I who am honored."

I carefully pinned the cherished heirloom on her soft lace blouse.

The gentle lady has since passed away. Whenever I watch the film, I push "pause" to catch a glimpse of Cornelia.

Kristen's and Amy's father, Charles McGary, was a local actor and an experienced film extra. He is the train conductor on the second leg of Ociee's trip. Completely contrary to his amiable personality, Chuck plays perfectly the role as an unfriendly chap. Sadly he, too, has died, but not before he proudly worked in a movie written, produced, directed, and filmed by two of his three daughters.

Writer, Writer

Mr. Tift and the Propsts

When our family was invited to become movie extras, we leapt at the opportunity.

During pre-production, Kristen called saying she'd found the perfect costume for our eight-month-old grandson, Loftin.

"Great," I squealed. "So this movie IS really happening."

"It's happening, all right," she laughed. "Loftin will look adorable in the antique boy's dress."

"That goes without saying."

"His is the first piece of clothing I've bought for the film."

During her long train trip, there is a montage of passengers who are seated across from Ociee to indicate the passage of time. Fittingly, Abigail, William, and Loftin play a young family.

Filming aboard the train presented unique challenges for the cast and crew. Obviously not authentic for the era, the modern and somewhat noisy air-conditioning would have to be turned off. The poor actors in heavy period costumes could relate to the discomfort of their fellow passengers in 1898.

Additionally, in order to be believable for the time period, shooting the montage had to be confined to a limited section of track. There could be no indication of the current day such as telephone poles, stop signs, automobiles, or any contemporary structures. Back and forth we traveled for three days!

To prevent Loftin from becoming overheated or sick from the train's motion, Jamey cared for him in the comfort of a nearby building. When it came time for his family's segment, the huge train came to a stop. Jamey passed Loftin through the window into the arms of his parents, who dressed their son in his tiny costume.

The vintage garment is proudly displayed in a shadow box in our home.

I had no dialogue for my acting debut. Good thing, I would have blown my lines.

Kristen instructed me to angrily elbow the fellow, who plays my husband, a dreadful snorer. She directed me to scowl as I attempt to wake him.

"But I've been grinning for weeks," I argued. "Besides, frowning makes me appear far too harsh."

At the scene's end, I sneaked in a subtle smile.

"Cut!" said Kristen. "Milam, the next time you do that, I'll have to replace you."

"Okay, you win."

To this day, I look away when my grumpy face appears on screen. I am, however, quite proud of my superb

Writer, Writer

elbow action. My snoring husband and the film's hairdresser, Phillip "Mr. P" Ivey, complained of noticeable bruising. I was pleased with my convincing performance.

Amanda and Jay participated in the film's closing scene, as did I. Amanda, looking cute as could be, thought her bonnet looked silly. Jay is very handsome in his costume as he strolls into Ociee Nash Day twirling a long walking stick. In my cameo shot, I grin from ear to ear.

The breakthrough star from the Propst family was Jamey. To prepare for his audition, the Man of My Dreams took acting lessons for a year at the Alliance Theater. Because there were so many accomplished stage performers trying out, he was concerned he'd not get to be in the movie. We were in Chattanooga at the Tennessee Valley Railroad when Jamey called.

"Baby Doll, I got the part! I'm Mr. Tift!"

Shortly after Ociee arrives in Asheville, she hurries to send a telegram to Papa. She approaches the telegraph window as the camera focuses on yet another scowl. It's not mine. This grumpy face belongs to my husband.

A natural like Woofer, Jamey spoke his six lines to perfection. His claim to fame is he is the only actor who did not require a second take. For weeks, it was like sleeping with a *Honeybaked Ham*. My husband bragged about the essential role he played.

"I was a central character."

"How so?"

"It's obvious. Up until my appearance, everyone had been reasonably kind to the little girl. I was the first person to introduce significant conflict. You notice how nastily I treat Ociee? It's a major turning point in the film."

I'm forever proud of Mr. Tift.

Writer, Writer

The Question

I'm often asked if I like the way *Charlotte Street* was turned into a movie.

The answer goes back to the first time I read the screenplay. I was in the study when Jamey walked by.

"I'm gonna cut the grass. How's the script?"

"It's wonderful!"

The lawn finished, the Man of My Dreams came back inside. I was stomping around the kitchen as furious as could be.

"They've written Aunt Mamie to be an aloof woman!"

Sensing danger, Jamey excused himself to his man cave in our basement. An hour later he cautiously climbed the stairs and slowly peeked around the corner. He found me weeping.

"Baby Doll, is it that bad?"

"It's perfect!"

I understood the McGary sisters introduced added conflict into the story by making Ociee's aunt a hard nut to crack. After all, a middle aged Victorian spinster, one who ran her own business and had never children, would have been uncomfortable in the role of a parent. Even though she had Ociee's best interest at heart and certainly wanted to help her widower brother, Mamie Nash found herself saddled with the responsibility of raising a rambunctious nine-year-old farm girl. Ociee had turned the maiden lady's life upside down. In my opinion, the screenwriters were right on target. It enhanced the storyline for Ociee to struggle to win over her aunt.

I enjoyed the McGary sisters' addition of historic figures. In *Forest Gump* like moments, Ociee rubs shoulders with Nellie Bly, President McKinley, and the Wright Brothers. Many a Ty Pennington fan delights seeing the dashing television star in the role of Wilbur Wright. I liked the idea so much, I even began including historic characters in my subsequent Ociee novels.

Another welcomed change to the original story was Kristen's and Amy's inventive way of bringing the gypsy back for final scene. Because he was one of my most cherished characters, it thrilled me to see them accomplish the feat. Following their lead, I had the gypsy mystically appear in *Ociee on Her Own*.

So my answer to the question, "Do you like how your book was treated?" is always a resounding yes!

Writer, Writer

Movie Premiere, June 1, 2003

The World Premiere of *The Adventures of Ociee Nash* was selected to kick off the Summer Movie Series at Atlanta's fabulous Fox Theater! Over the moon with anticipation, I thought the night would never get here.

Every day leading up to June 1, we heard from more people who were coming to the premier. They weren't all from Atlanta either. In fact, most of the out-of-town folks on our Christmas card list ordered tickets, made hotel reservations, and were busily packing their suitcases. Between the McGary's family and supporters and ours, we filled the Georgian Terrace Hotel.

Just before 7 o'clock, everyone gathered in the lobby to line up for the Red Carpet. Victorian costumes put aside, the movie's stars were magnificent in their stunning gowns and handsome tuxedos. The rest of us looked mighty fine, too. Jamey was all decked out in his tux; while, after days of shopping for the perfect thing, I finally decided on a bright pink and cream tea-length dress. I proudly wore B's cameo.

A large entourage of her family and friends from Cumming surrounded a sparkling Skyler. Bill's contingent from Montgomery excitedly congratulated their young actor for doing such a terrific job as Ociee's brother, Ben.

Beverly and Tom Key, along with their three sons, greeted his fellow stage actors from the film including Janice Akers, Daniel Burnley, Jill Jane Clements, Sean Daniels, Bart Hansard, George Lawes, John Lawhorn, Geoff McKnight and Mary Welch Rogers. Ty Pennington definitely set off swoons when he made his appearance.

Traffic was brought to a halt as a red carpet was rolled across Peachtree Street. Kristen and Amy, equally splendid in their stunning black outfits, called everyone to attention.

"Ready?"

"Yes!" we shouted.

"Let's go!"

I licked lipstick off my teeth and took Jamey's arm. The cast and crew, the director and the producer, this writer, and a parade of Ociee fans burst through the hotel doors. A bluegrass band played as it lead us through the jubilant crowd of cheering moviegoers.

Jamey squeezed my hand. "Baby Doll, this damn sure trumps our wedding!"

Hundreds and hundreds of people, for as far as we could see, were taking pictures, waving, shouting, and applauding. And this was before they watched the movie! Jamey and I were dancing and whirling around shaking everyone's hands. He and I hugged people until our shoulders ached.

His sister, Maryetta, organized a delegation of Propsts, Loftins, and Buchanans from the four corners of Alabama including her three children Danny, JEP, and Mary Shea, and many of their family members. Jamey's thoughtful people wanted to fill the void left by Mary and Ed Propst, who were too infirmed and elderly to travel.

My family was well represented, too. My cousin Kay from Memphis and her daughter Kathleen from Bloomington, Indiana, were on hand; as were my grandmother's Nash connections, Sheila and Fred. They drove from Houston making a swing through Fort Walton Beach to pick up his eighty-nine-year-old mother, Ociee Nash Robnett. Named for my grandmother at the insistence of her father Fred Nash, Ociee Robnett enthusiastically approved the choice of the actor who plays Fred.

"Charles Nuckols does a perfect job capturing Dad's personality. Handsome as could be, my father was the strong silent type, exactly as he is portrayed."

In the audience were twenty-five of my classmates from St. Pius X High Catholic High School. Our class had graduated on that very stage June 1, 1963, forty years ago to the day. One class member was Betty Ann. I'd written the characters of Elizabeth Murphy and her mother Frances as a tribute to BA and her mother. Jasmine Sky, who plays

Elizabeth, was thrilled to meet the inspiration for her character.

Famous people in the spotlight will often say they are humbled at such an event. Not me! The night of the premier, I was euphoric. I squealed and kissed and embraced and raved and carried on like a Jack Russell terrier on steroids. Just before the curtain rose, Kristen introduced me. I stood and turned in a full circle taking a mental photo of every person in the enormous theater.

My eye caught Jerry Lee's. He winked at me.

Jamey and I were seated behind Amanda and Jay and their dates. William sat next to me. On his side were Abigail and her sister, Rachel, and their parents, JoAnne and Alan.

I flashed hot and cold with anticipation as the curtain slowly began to rise revealing the Fox's giant screen. Skyler and Woofer are dashing across an open field of flowers as *The Adventures of Ociee Nash* appears. Everyone started whistling, whoopin,' and hollarin'!

It was total madness, and I relished every moment.

"Based on a novel by Milam McGraw Propst."

I still tremble recalling those huge letters spelling out my name. This was truly the ultimate by-line.

I touched Jamey's arm and whispered. "Almost everybody we care about is in this theater." For me, that realization captured the real treasure of the night.

Writer, Writer

As the film ran, the cheering continued with ongoing whistles and shouts. We couldn't always hear the dialogue or the fine score by Van Dyke Parks. But everyone was having too much fun to object.

The countless voices of the extras echoed, "There I am!"

"Look for me on the train!"

"See, dear, that's me walking behind Mr. Lynch's buggy."

The ending credits ran to more excitement as names of the cast and crew began appearing. Significant in the list was film editor, Amy Linton. Then the actors themselves walked on stage to a curtain call and a standing ovation. Ociee was a hit!

I made my way through well-wishers and to more kind kudos in the lobby. I was especially pleased when Jamey's cousin, Jerry Loftin, approached me. He and his wife, Joyce had traveled from Nicholsville with his brother, Sam.

Grinning broadly Jerry said, "I really enjoyed your picture show, Milam, especially the first part. The farm reminded me of home."

"It was your home, Jerry. I was writing about Nicholsville when I wrote *Charlotte Street*. Thank you for coming all this way."

Jerry chuckled, "I didn't know Jamey was an actor!"

We both laughed.

I dropped by the reception in the Fox's Egyptian Ballroom, where many in the audience had gathered. I chatted, posed for pictures, and lapped up their kind words. Surely my grandmother was somewhere looking on!

Other special people were celebrating at a second party at our hotel. I excused myself and walked alone down the theater's arcade.

"How about this, B?"

I spotted the gypsy's wagon. There stood Anthony in costume greeting young fans and signing autographs. I rushed over and kissed his cheek.

I stopped in front of a display case featuring dresses worn by Skyler and Jasmine, and once again whispered words of gratitude to my grandmother for her story.

I thought back to jotting initial ideas on my tablet and typing early dialogue on a portable typewriter. I remembered editing the first chapters on our old Apple computer. I envisioned its Arial font on the tiny eight-inch screen.

I thought about the rejection letters, a stack two inches high. I'd recently burned the dern things in a silly ceremony. Included was Mr. Levin's.

Writer, Writer

I thought about Marc's calling to say Mercer wanted to publish my book.

I thought about the life changing lunch with Amy and Kristen, and my gratitude to the talented sisters for their hard work and perseverance.

The red carpet rolled up, I was jaywalking across Peachtree, when I heard two familiar voices.

"It was wonderful!" beamed my friends, Ginger and Mary Alyce, as they ran up with a congratulatory hugs.

I did feel like somebody pretty special.

Ociee's Poem

A letter arrived the following week. My cousin Ociee thanked us for her exciting trip. Quite the Belle of the Ball, she dressed in blue with matching shoes and purse. A retired business woman, Ociee Robnett is our family's historian and a poet, as well. With her permission, I'm including her poem. In it she speaks with the voice of my grandmother.

Star Light, Star Bright

by

Ociee Annette Nash Robnett

It was just by chance that she happened to see

Down below on a theatre marquee.

It was dark, yet a blue cloud wafted by

And there came clear breaks in a darkening sky.

"Oh my! Did I see what I think I did?"

Then a darker cloud came, and the light place was hid.

She waited and when a wide opening came

Was speechless when sure she'd seen her old name!

"What in the old world could this possibly be?

Could someone down there be summoning me?"

Then an angel appeared and said, "Don't you recall

The dear little girl who grew up fine and tall

And heard as you told of your life down there,

So she put it in book, so it could be shared!"

"Then there were others, both clever and bright

Who filmed what your granddaughter did write.

Still others who are versed in the acting art

Came forth to play friends and family parts.

You said you missed your dad, who's now up here, too.

But a fine man played like he was "Papa" to you.

And Benny? Well, he didn't stay a small boy

But while he was there, shared your childhood joy.

Brother Fred lived to see you happily grown

And added some stories for *Ociee on Her Own*!

"My goodness!" the first observer declared

"But I still say, what's going on down there?"

"Well, I'll tell you," the clever angel explained,

We both recall things from before we came

And that's one thing that I happen to know,

Writer, Writer

The lights you see are at a picture show.
Folks crowding there to get inside to see
What a brave little girl you used to be!"
"Pshaw! Oh my. I'm shocked to see it like this
But I'll admit that's it's nice to be missed.
I'll go on now, get busy, as I should
But I hope things she recalled were just the good!"

For Dessert, our Trip to New Orleans

After the ecstasy of the premier, I tried to settle back into a normal routine. But experiencing such an electrifying event is akin to hosting a huge wedding. There's a let down afterwards. I was in a complete funk.

Kristen McGary called from New Orleans, where she was working on a television movie about Elvis Presley. Appropriately called *Elvis*, the film would earn four Golden Globes.

She mentioned having some time off, and said she was lonesome for Jamey, Jerry Lee, and me. She enticed me further saying her co-worker Brian, who is a New Orleans native, offered to take us places the average tourist seldom sees. How could we not go? I pressured Jamey into driving down the following weekend, and Jerry Lee came along with us.

What writer wouldn't relish a trip to New Orleans? Out of my funk I burst!

We stopped in Fairhope for lunch with friends, Genia and her mother Eugenia, a well known painter whose work hangs in our home. The charming Alabama retreat breeds artists. Beverly Key also honed her talents by the shores of Mobile Bay. Our pleasant break in Fairhope set the perfect mood for our weekend. We said goodbye and headed south for the last three-hour leg.

Writer, Writer

Jamey mentioned being drowsy, so Jerry Lee offered to drive. I kept my seat as the Man of My Dreams crawled in back for a snooze. He was snoring away, and Jerry Lee and I were deep in conversation about our upcoming adventure. We were all but airborne as we crossed the long bridge over Lake Pontchartrain.

Suddenly my husband jerked awake.

"Damn, Jerry Lee!" he screamed. "Slow down!"

"Lord, I'm sorry, Jamey," he said pumping the brakes. "I must have been doing 110 MPH!"

"Jerry Lee, man, my tires ain't that good."

Jamey's old car, a black Mercury Marquis, was the same model as many police cars. Local officers must have assumed we were members of their team.

Kristen kept her promise and some. Our weekend was filled with fun, laughter, and yummy, yummy New Orleans cuisine. Neither did Brian disappoint. He drove us all throughout his city showing off its welcoming parks, churches and schools, tree shaded boulevards, and gorgeous homes in the Garden District. We dined at scrumptious eateries including my favorite, Jacamo's.

As we rode through the French Quarter, Brian slowed our car to point out an old apartment house.

"Tennessee Williams once lived there. As you can see, the building is currently under renovation. Sorry, but we can't go inside."

Jerry Lee was crushed. So devoted is he to the famous American playwright and author, he keeps Tennessee's photo enshrined next to his computer for creative inspiration.

Later in the day, when back on our own, we walked around the square in front of St. Louis Cathedral. Delighting in booth after booth of artists and craftsman, Jamey surprised me by purchasing a colorful oil painting to commemorate our trip.

We came upon a Rastafarian, a man who interpreted chicken bones to discern the future. Jerry Lee couldn't resist and sat down for a reading. The mystical man with dreadlocks shook the bones, dumped them onto his table, and turned his eyes peering directly into Jerry Lee's.

The Rastafarian told our friend that an old lady was standing at his side. He described her as a mountain woman with long gray hair cascading down her back to well below her hips. His description matched perfectly that of Jerry Lee's recently departed grandmother. Her prized hair, lost in her courageous fight against cancer, was restored. Jerry Lee was shaking all over.

All of us were unnerved, even more so when the man began to list Jerry Lee's unique personality traits. He

Writer, Writer

revealed things about our friend he could not have guessed correctly. Jerry Lee was brought to tears. As were Kristen and I.

The next evening, we returned to have the fortune teller reveal futures for Jamey and Kristen.

"Not me, I'm too chicken to have chicken bones read!" I laughed. I wasn't really trying to be funny, it was the truth. I'd started thinking about our scary old house on Hector Avenue.

We returned to the Rastafarian's spot, but he wasn't there, so we walked around the square in search of him. The man had disappeared, as if into thin air.

Already feeling mystical and weird, we decided to take a French Quarter ghost tour. It was what we expected, sort of spooky with a good measure of camp and cheesiness, as the guide told us about murders, voodoo, suicides, and vampires. Our festive mood turned sour when a young man, who'd evidently steadied his fears with booze, threw up by my foot. I've never been one who sympathizes with alcohol induced vomiting.

We left the ghost tour and strolled along talking about what we might do next. We'd just rounded a corner near St. Ann Street, when Jerry Lee suddenly took off in a mad dash.

"Tennessee's apartment is near here!" He hollered over his shoulder.

Kristen ran after Jerry Lee. I looked at Jamey.

"Go on, Baby Doll. I'll catch up with you crazy people in a minute."

Arriving at the building, Kristen gave the front door a gentle push. It swung open, and we tiptoed inside. There were voices coming from the floor above us. We crept forward. Before us was a long circular stairway.

Jerry Lee exclaimed, "Can't you see old Tennessee, drunk as hell, staggering up those stairs!"

Like the vomiting, I also don't do well with drunks wobbling on steps. But I let go of my hang-ups and laughed hysterically at his hilarious reenactment of the esteemed playwright's clumsy crawl up to his apartment.

Jamey arrived, panting and concerned. Very concerned. "Y'all can't go up there!"

"Why not?"

"Well? What the hell."

My husband pushed past Kristen, Jerry Lee, and me and headed to the second floor. The next thing we knew the workmen were laughing and talking with Jamey like long lost Army buddies.

My husband could make friends with an axe murderer.

The smell of marijuana permeated the building. The giggly painters were more than happy to accept Jamey's

Writer, Writer

$20 donation. They pocketed the money and opened the door.

"We're in the same space where Tennessee lived and worked," whispered Jerry Lee as if we were in a holy place.

"Look at my arm," I said. "It's covered with goose bumps."

Kristen stood silent in awe.

I noticed a second door and gave it a nudge.

"Come in here, y'all!"

Standing at the window, we gazed out across the street and saw what looked exactly like a stage set for *A Streetcar Named Desire*.

"STELLLLLLLA!" We shouted in unison.

For us, there was no question; Tennessee Williams had written his world famous play in that room. I shivered with the realization the playwright's feet had paced back and forth on those very floors. Employing his singular creative technique, did the brilliant writer gaze at those same structures as he struggled to craft a perfect sentence for *Stanley Kowalski* to spit out?

Our improbable experience in the French Quarter apartment was spellbinding. Our being there was unexpected, random, funny with the hippy dippy painters, and so personal for Kristen, Jerry Lee, Jamey, and me.

It was the Vatican.

It was Mecca.

It was an author's heaven.

Writer, Writer

Charlie's Right

On our last full day, Kristen asked if there were anything else we might want to do.

"I'd like to ride through Metarie and see if I can find my old house," I suggested. "It's on Hector Avenue."

"Let's go."

I didn't tell anyone, not even Jamey; but I did see the house. At least, I saw where our house used to be. The bungalow was gone. In its place was a MacMansion. I was pleased the new house was big; because its enormity squashed, once and for all, the coal bin monster ghost.

I squeezed shut my eyes and released forever the monster and the wolf. As we passed slowly by not once but twice, I thought about the good moments.

I remembered riding on my wooden horse on the front walk.

I remembered being snuggled by Momma after the tree fell.

I remembered rushing to meet B as she walked home from her bus stop.

I remembered Creola Moon telling her stories.

I remembered drawing hopscotch with chalk, and watching Daddy push his lawnmower. I remembered where he stopped to wave at me.

Charlie Chaplin was right when he said, "Life is a tragedy when seen in close-up, but a comedy in long-shot."

It pleases me to learn Charlie Chaplin was born in 1889, the same year as my grandmother. A quarter of a century after her death, my grandmother continues to influence my writing. On the morning of January 17, 2013, Mr. Chaplin's quote changed the focus of my book. Had B lead me to his words?

In its inception, this book had begun as a serious look at how creativity can arise from trauma and family dysfunction. I'd sent it to Marc Jolley, who wanted better from me. I talked with my editor, Letitia Sweitzer, who suggested I might try an entirely different theme.

The morning following my meeting with Letitia, I came upon this perfect quote from Mr. Chaplin. Ultimately, I rewrote the book tossing out page after page of hard work. As I was making the daunting decision to change directions, January 17 jumped off the page at me. Familiar? Oh yes.

January 17, 1998, marks my mother's death. Momma had certainly played a vital role in this rewrite. She added the funny stuff.

Just like Charlie said, "In long-shot, it's a comedy."

##############################

A THANK YOU NOTE

My husband kindly read every word of this book's original manuscript. Thank you, Jamey, for everything you do to support my work. I do love you so.

There are many others I'd like to recognize, who either planned book events or had something to do with the Ociee movie. Each and every person matters to me.

Jackie White, dear friend, author, survivor, and fellow traveler.

Summer Paul, artist, entertainer, sweet young friend, and the talented creator of the cover for *Writer, Writer*

Brian Aubitz, patient printer, lovely man.

Letitia Sweitzer, brave editor, the lady who encouraged me to pitch the trash and focus on a more comfortable theme.

Kristen McGary Handziuk and Amy McGary for making your film.

Jackie Brown, Pam Weeks, and Sandy Aubitz, proofreaders and longtime fans.

Beverly Key, a major *key* to my endeavors.

Florence Walsh, whose eyes spotted many a wrongly placed semi-colon.

Betty Ann Colley, whose ears never seem to tire of my ramblings.

Jerry Lee Davis, a member of our family, a spiritual guru, an angel.

Marc Jolley, Ph.D., a hero for me and Ociee.

Bella the Dog, Nestle's successor in walking with me and listening.

Party givers and special supporters:

Terry Akins, Marilyn Bailey, Kay Beebe, Ave Bransford, Mary and Marvin Brantley, Jackie Brown, JoAnn Brown, Maryetta Buchanan, Kathy Brush, Carolyn Carter, Becky Crum, Cynthia and Bill Davis, Diane Dean, Elizabeth Ellett, Jerrie and George Elliott, Judy and Bill Ekiss, Patty Engstrom, Dana Evans, Margaret Farrell, Betty George, Susan and Sam Jannetta, Jody Johnson, Linda Kelleher, Nora King, Valiere Kuffrey, Linda Lacey, Susan Lindsey, Marsha Little, Susan Lundy, Popsie and Don Lynch, Patty Malec, Starr Millen, Margaret Mittiga, LaWana Moroski, Phyllis Perry, Helen Reppert, Bev Riccardi, Dick Schweitzer, Judi Schubert, Kate and Lou Shilling, Sue Smith, Wylda Smith, Jeff Stives, Nancy Stone, Sandy Taylor, Jane Tonning, Dannie Walther, Pam Weeks, Francine White, Jean Wilsterman, Marybeth Woodward, and Marilynn and Ron Winston.

Writer, Writer

Actors in *the Adventures of Ociee Nash*
Skyler Day, Mare Winningham and Keith Carradine, Tom Key, Anthony Rodriguez, and Jamey Propst, along with a number of fine Atlanta Stage performers in the Ociee film which included: Janice Akers, Daniel Burnley, Jill Jane Clements, Sean Daniels, Bart Hansard, George Lawes, John Lawhorn, Charles McGary, Geoff McKnight, Ty Pennington, Mary Welch Rogers, and Donna Wright.

Movie Extras in the Ociee Movie:
Mary and Marvin Brantley, Jackie Brown, Clara Croxton, Cynthia and Bill Davis, Jerry Lee Davis, Elizabeth Ellett, Ryan Flanders, Cornelia Jolly, Marc and Patrick Jolley, Christa Leveto, Bob Mayers, Delores and Chuck McGary, Kellie McGary, Amanda Propst, Abigail, William and Loftin Propst, Jay Propst, Babs Rymer, Wylda and Cantey Smith, Pam and Kelsey Weeks, Janelle and Bob Whetstone.

Movie Crew: Not only those I happened to photograph; many, many more worked hard on the film. To all, I remain most grateful.
First of all, Steve Dirkes, for starting the ball rolling, and Dennis Adams, Robert Ballentine, Jerry Lee Davis, Ann Halloran, Margaret Hungerford, Jennifer Ivey, Amy and

Greg Linton, Sarah Massaro, Susan Mickey, Bart Patton, Judy Ponder, Stephanie Ryan, Carol Sadler, Roger Sherer, Sue Ellen Smith, Jaye Walker, and Angie Woodard, and the young student's tutor, Connie Baker.

I sincerely hope no one has been overlooked. If you have, please forgive me!